He watched her ⬛⬛⬛⬛⬛⬛⬛⬛⬛
swallowed. Her ⬛⬛⬛⬛⬛⬛⬛

Searching for a way t⬛⬛⬛⬛⬛⬛⬛⬛⬛
had an idea. "How about if I hang around Saturday morning and help you and Jolene with your community swap meet?"

He couldn't read her thoughts, but he sensed her heightened tension. "I'd find ways to occupy myself, and help you. Don't you trust me?"

She shifted her position on the stump and glanced away, clearly uncomfortable. "I trust you," she said at last.

Trace rolled his shoulders. "You're a smart lady."

She looked down at her overalls and snickered. "Some lady I am. More like a hillbilly tomboy."

With that she swung her legs around and hopped off the stump.

"Are you done frog hunting?" he asked.

She didn't look up. "Yep."

He slid off the stump and reached for the handle of her frog bucket. "I'll carry this for—"

He slipped as he picked up the heavier-than-expected bucket, and a foot plunged into the murky pond water. He yelped.

Now she did look up, and a beautiful smile lit her face.

He extended a hand for an assist but she ignored it. And laughed.

HELEN GRAY

grew up in a small Missouri town and married her pastor. While working alongside her husband in his ministry, she had three children, taught school, became an amateur ventriloquist and directed/accompanied church music programs. Now that she is retired and the children are grown, she has resumed the writing she began when they were small.

Her stories are meant to honor God and depict Christian lives and problems as she knows and observes them. If her writing in even a small way touches others, she considers it a blessing and thanks God for the opportunity.

HELEN GRAY

Ozark Sweetheart

HEARTSONG
PRESENTS

Recycling programs
for this product may
not exist in your area.

TM LOVE INSPIRED BOOKS

ISBN-13: 978-0-373-48701-1

OZARK SWEETHEART

www.Harlequin.com

Printed in U.S.A.

Therefore I say unto you, take no thought for your life, what ye shall eat, or what ye shall drink; nor yet for your body, what ye shall put on. Is not the life more than meat, and the body than raiment?
—*Matthew* 6:25

Chapter 1

Missouri, 1930

Callie Blake picked up a couple more sticks of firewood from the slab pile and added them to her load. Arms full, she rounded the sawdust pile near the family sawmill and headed for the house. She twisted her head, wishing she had a free hand to wipe the sweat that trickled from beneath her bonnet and dampened the collar of her blue cotton dress. The smell of fresh sawdust permeated the still, parched air.

The family dog lay panting in the sweltering shade of a huge oak tree, his tongue hanging out. The calendar said today was the third of September, but the heat of August persisted in the Missouri Ozarks.

The sound of a motor drew her attention to the road.

A 1927 Chevrolet truck slowed and pulled into the strip of ground between the road and the yard.

Callie paused as the visitor got out of the truck and came closer. Then she got her first look at his face.

Trace Gentry.

The sight of him sent her tumbling back in time. He was as tall as she remembered, six foot or a little more, and as good-looking as ever. His dark brown hair held just a hint of curl, and deep-set blue eyes made hearts flutter—including Callie's, once upon a time. Time and trials had changed him from a "cute" boy to a lean, muscular man. A heart-stoppingly handsome man.

He carried himself with assurance and always seemed at ease with everyone. Nobody else had ever fascinated Callie the way he did, or sent her stomach into somersaults at the mere thought of him. Or been so far from her world.

Time stood still as he came closer. Suddenly his eyes collided with hers in recognition. She struggled for control and forced the shock from her expression.

"Callie?" Surprise colored the word.

She nodded, held mute at his sudden appearance.

"Are you just visiting, or have you moved back here?" His voice was deep and smooth.

"I came home six months ago." She had to force the words past numb lips.

As a child—and as she grew older—she had adored him from a distance. In high school he had only seen her as the poor little Blake girl he had once felt sorry for. Trace had dated Joanna Michaels, a girl his own age who had been a perfect match for him, and Callie had put away her childish fairy-tale dreams.

"Are you looking for Dad?"

He gave her a breathtaking smile. "I want to get some advice from him and order wood to build a display case in the showroom."

She tipped her head, slowly regaining her composure. "For all your trophies?"

A smile hovered around his mouth. "No, for my license plate collection."

"He was at the sawmill, but the steam engine stopped running a few minutes ago. If he's not right there, he may have gone to the barn." Callie indicated with a jerk of her head where the engine sat just beyond the second sawdust pile. She clutched the load of wood tighter and hooked her hands together around it to keep it from slipping from her tired arms.

Trace looked at the wood in her arms. "You're busy. I'll go on down and find him."

He moved toward the barn, and Callie continued to the house. Just then a movement to her right caught her attention. Her brothers, Riley, one year older than her at twenty-three, and eighteen-year-old Delmer, sprinted from the barn and cut across the backyard to the other side of the house where the buckboard sat, a team of horses already hitched to it.

Callie's mouth tightened in irritation. Ducking out on their chores again. Why did she have to be the only one who took care of everything? Would she never be free to have a life of her own?

Callie picked up her pace and opened her mouth to yell that Mom needed more wood for the cookstove. But the sound of another approaching motor brought her to a halt.

A black car pulled to the side of the road. A man in black pants, shirt and hat got out and rounded the front of the vehicle, its motor still running. She froze in her tracks. *Could it be?* The familiar-looking man stopped at the ditch and stared across it at Riley and Delmer. A bolt of fear zinged up her spine as he studied them from beneath the shield of his hat brim. He said something she couldn't hear.

The wood nearly slipped out of her hands, but Callie tightened her arms just in time to keep from dropping it. *Could it be him? How could he have found her? Oh, please, no.*

Callie edged backward around the corner of the house, keeping her eyes glued to the man and her brothers. Intent on each other, they hadn't noticed her. The man suddenly reached behind him. When his hand came back around, he was pointing a gun at the boys. Cold, paralyzing fear held Callie's feet rooted to the ground.

Run. Move—before they're both dead.

A shot rang out, and Riley collapsed. In a flash the man swung his arm around toward Delmer, who flung himself to the ground in a fast rolling movement. More shots fired, bullets hitting the dirt around him.

Callie screamed and broke into a run, nearly tripping over the wood that fell at her feet. Acting on sheer instinct, she flung a chunk at the man. It landed several feet short of him. Still running, she fired another missile from the middle of the yard. It bounced off his ankle. The man hesitated and turned, giving her a partial view of a face identical to the one in her nightmares.

Regaining her balance, Callie hurled another stick, then another, while running up to within a few feet of him. When a stick of wood pelted him in the neck, he whirled and ran back to his car.

Delmer scrambled on hands and knees to where Riley lay. The car sputtered and rumbled away. Callie had a fleeting impulse to chase after it, but Riley was her first concern. Heart pounding, she dropped the last of the wood and landed on her knees next to the boys.

"Is he…" With her heart in her throat, she couldn't finish the question.

Delmer yanked Riley's shirt back, and blood poured from his chest. Delmer pressed a hand over the wound.

Dear God, please don't let us lose another brother. Please, please don't let that happen.

Their mother and youngest sister, Clementine, came running across the yard to join them. Callie jumped up. "I'm going to get some towels," she shouted, breaking into a run. In the kitchen she grabbed the towel from the nail by the door and yanked a dishtowel from the supply cabinet. Then she ran back to Riley and skidded to a breathless halt on her knees beside him. She pressed the towels over the wound.

"We have to get him to a doctor," she gasped, trying to ignore her mother's pitiful moans at her side. *Lord, why didn't You let me get enough saved to buy a car?*

"What happened?" Trace Gentry came at a run around the corner of the house.

Callie pointed at the car headed up the road. "A man drove up and shot Riley. We have to get him to a doctor."

Trace squatted and grasped Riley's feet. "Let's put him in my truck. It's faster."

Delmer hooked his hands under his brother's shoulders, and they carried him the twenty yards to the truck and eased him into the open end of the bed. Heart pounding, Callie followed them, and nearly forgot to breathe when a soft moan came from Riley. "I'll ride back here with him."

Callie crawled up beside Riley and placed his head

in her lap, while Delmer stayed at his feet. *Thank You, Lord, that Trace was here with his truck.*

As the truck took off, Callie ran one hand over Riley's forehead and pressed the towels over the wound with the other. "Riley, Riley," she crooned. "You know you drive me crazy at times, but you also know I love you. Where were you guys going that was so important?" She feared that she knew.

"You look too much like me." She groaned and ran her eyes over his oval face and black hair that matched her own. Tears coursed down her cheeks, knowing that very likeness might have cost him his life. How had that man found her?

She leaned forward. "Don't you dare die on me, big brother. Don't you dare. Do you hear me?" Pain cut through her heart.

Please don't let him come back. God, hasn't my family suffered enough? Grief and backbreaking work have aged Mom and Dad so much since Everett's death. Lord, I'm sorry I neglected You for so long.

"Did you hear me, Riley?" she demanded fiercely. "You are *not* going to die."

The three-mile ride to Deer Lick seemed to take forever. Her neck grew tired from looking every direction for the gunman. By the time they reached the four-way stop sign at the center of town, Callie was holding on to her nerves by a thread.

The horn sounded continuously as the truck careened left, sped to the middle of the block and stopped in front of the drugstore on the west side of Main Street. Delmer hopped to the street and ran inside the store. As he passed the soda fountain to the doctor's office in the back, his panicked shout carried to the street. "My brother's been shot. He needs a doctor."

The gray-haired Dr. Randolph came running out with his nurse, then removed Callie's hand from Riley's chest and made sure he was breathing. "Help me get him inside," he ordered gruffly.

"Careful now," he cautioned as Trace helped him carry Riley up onto the sidewalk. They were just easing through the door when the buckboard came racing up the street. Callie's father jumped from the seat. A stocky man with broad shoulders and sturdy legs, he wore a look of sheer panic.

"Clem said Riley's been shot. Who did it?" he demanded, his face flushed. When he got no answer, he jerked off his dirty hat, leaving his thinning gray hair plastered to his head.

"We don't know," Mom said, resisting his effort to take her place. He walked beside her into the doctor's quarters where a strong antiseptic smell greeted them.

"Please have a seat, everyone." The nurse motioned to the sofa and chairs in the small waiting room. "We'll call as soon as we have everything under control." She, the doctor and Trace disappeared into the examining room with Riley.

Callie took one of the two chairs by the door. She wiped her hands on her dress and clasped them tightly together to control their trembling. Moments later Mom, Dad and Trace returned, firmly shut out of the doctor's office. When Trace sat in the chair next to her and their arms brushed, Callie stiffened and edged away. The tingle that shot through her made heat rise in her face. She forced herself to ignore his presence beside her—and keep her mind on Riley.

Leon Gentry, the city marshal and Trace's brother, appeared in the doorway and dipped his head in a polite greeting. "Hi, folks. I heard y'all come tearing into town and recognized Trace's truck. Care to tell me what happened?"

Callie eased back into the sofa and did her best to be invisible.

As soon as she'd graduated from high school, she had gone to Saint Louis to work and send money to her mother so the family wouldn't go hungry. That had ended abruptly six months ago. As the weeks passed, she had begun to breathe easier. Now this.

The partially visible face of the gunman filled her mind. The brief glimpse she had gotten looked like the man she had run from in Saint Louis. She tried to deny it. Maybe someone else had been after the boys because of something related to the bootlegging she knew they'd been involved with. But if it *was* him, how had he found her?

The marshal's eyes pierced all of them. "Was he alone?"

Mom's eyes darted to her offspring. "Delmer and Callie wuz there."

He focused on Delmer. "Tell me about it."

Delmer swallowed, his Adam's apple bobbing. "This car came up and stopped. A man got out. He asked our names. I said, 'Who wants to know?' He looked at us real mean, then he stared at Riley and said, 'You're the one.' He pulled out a gun and shot Riley. Then he tried to shoot me, but I rolled away."

"Do you have any idea why?"

Delmer shook his head. "No."

The marshal glowered. "You're sure?"

The doctor emerged at that moment, his manner brusque. "The bullet just missed his heart. I think he'll make it."

A breath of relief whooshed from Callie, leaving her weak.

"He's unconscious but fairly stable. You may go to him, but not everyone at once." He looked at Dad and Mom. "You two first."

As soon as her parents disappeared through a door, Marshal Gentry shifted his attention to Trace and Callie. He started to speak, but hesitated for a moment, as if uncertain about questioning his brother.

"Why don't we walk up the street to Trace's office at the car dealership? It's closer than the jail and more private than this. You won't be gone long." His tone suggested they should not refuse his request.

Without comment Callie and Delmer followed the Gentry brothers across the street and up the sidewalk to the Gentry Chevrolet building. Callie had to tamp down a twinge of envy that the Gentrys still had a livelihood and such a nice business, unlike most of her friends and family members. And the whole place stirred too many memories. That ride to town years ago had been too much like the one today. She plucked at the skirt of her dirty dress.

"Do you know any reason someone would shoot Riley?"

Delmer's eyes darted to the door, as if he wanted to escape through it. "No, I don't," he practically shouted, his face nearly matching his red hair.

"Tell me again exactly what the man said," Leon ordered.

Delmer clenched his fists. After a few deep breaths he

seemed to calm a bit and met the marshal's gaze. "Like I told you, this guy drove up, got out of the car without shutting off the motor and came to the edge of the road. He asked our names, but we didn't tell him. Figured it wasn't none a' his business, since we didn't know his. He pulled out a gun, shot my brother and took off. And I was too scared and worried about Riley to go catch him," he choked.

Leon turned his attention to his brother. "How did you get involved in this?"

"I went out there to order wood for a display case I plan to build back there for my license plate collection." Trace nodded toward the back wall as he explained what he'd seen.

"So you didn't see what happened or who did it."

"Nothing but the car. It was a 1928 Dodge Coupe."

Leon made a note. "Any little detail might help. What about you?"

He had switched his focus to Callie so quickly that she blinked in surprise.

"Tell us what you saw."

Callie drew a deep breath and fought for control. She ran her tongue over dry lips. "I came around the house just as the car pulled up. The boys had started to get in the buckboard, and I meant to speak to them. But when the car stopped, I backed up so I wouldn't interrupt."

"Could you hear what the man said?"

She shook her head. "No, I backed out of sight, figuring it was someone the boys knew." She couldn't bring herself to explain what she feared.

The marshal gave Delmer a grim scowl. "I've heard there are some rough characters hanging out in our woods, buying stuff from some of our locals. You wouldn't know anything about that, would you?" Strong meaning laced the words.

Delmer's Adam's apple bobbed again. "No, sir." The response was low and unconvincing.

Callie's heart ached. Of course the marshal knew about the local stills. The boys had money lately because they had gotten involved in bootlegging. After the crash of 1929, poverty and hard times made people willing to do most anything to get their hands on some money, even forsake their Christian principles.

Marshal Gentry's gaze turned speculative on Callie. "Did the man look familiar to you?"

Callie swallowed hard and tightened her entwined fingers. She couldn't lie, but she couldn't get the whole story past her lips. What if she told him she feared the gunman had shot the wrong person? It might not have been him. "I may have seen him somewhere, but I don't know his name." That was the absolute truth.

"Then why are you so scared?"

She stiffened her shoulders and raised her chin. "Marshal Gentry, I saw a man shoot my brother. He could come back and shoot more of my family. Why wouldn't I be scared?"

She shot to her feet and marched to the door. "I have to get back to Riley."

To her surprise, Trace followed her. Delmer started to, as well, but the marshal halted him. "Sit down, young man. I'm not done with you."

Callie met her youngest brother's eyes and nodded that he should cooperate, then she turned and left the building.

Trace caught up with her. They walked in silence to the end of the block before Callie came to an abrupt halt and faced him—then wished she hadn't. He was taller than she remembered. Of course, she had never stood this close to him. That is, not since the age of seven.

"Why are you trailing after me?" she demanded, wishing she didn't always feel at such a disadvantage around him.

He touched a detaining hand to her shoulder, his eyes going even darker. The late-afternoon sun made her squint up at him. "I wanted to talk to you. I think you know more than you're telling. What are you really afraid of?"

Callie jutted her chin a notch higher and kept her face as impassive as possible. "You heard what I told your brother. A gangster shot my brother and is running loose around here."

His eyes narrowed. "Gangster? You didn't say anything about a gangster before."

She attempted to shrug it off, regretting the slip of tongue. "He reminded me of pictures I've seen of gangsters, dressed in black and carrying guns. That's all I meant. And it's improper for us to be out here together. You have a fiancée, and I'm sure she wouldn't approve."

"I don't have a fiancée."

Chapter 2

Callie stared at him, her eyes rounded in shock. "You're not engaged to Beulah Parker?" she asked after several moments.

"I am not. We broke up this past week."

Her mouth moved soundlessly, as if struggling to grasp what he had said. "I'm sorry. I—"

"Don't be," he cut off her words of sympathy. "I made a mistake."

"I've made my share of those," she said, chin up, her expression even. "I have to get back to my family."

Head high, she resumed her march back to the doctor's office.

Trace watched her for a moment, and then strode back to his office, deeply disturbed by what had happened to Riley Blake, and unable to prevent a mental comparison between Callie Blake and his ex-fiancée. Beulah might dress nicer than Callie Blake, and the name Beulah might mean *beautiful,* but he had learned that she was not a beautiful person. He couldn't believe how good it felt to be free.

After his first love Joanna's death, too numb with grief to have any interest in another relationship, he had buried himself in work. He was proud of the success he had achieved as his dad gave him more and more authority, making improvements and expanding sales. He also liked the affluence that accompanied success and had plans for further growth in both the business and his savings account. But he had hard work ahead of him if he continued to succeed in these terrible times.

During a period of acute loneliness after years alone, he had let his parents nudge him into going out with Beulah Parker, the daughter of their longtime close friends. He had been fond of Beulah at the time, so when she asked him if he intended to marry her, he had foolishly said yes. He had regretted it almost immediately. Catching her at the movie theater smooching with another man had been a painful betrayal, but a welcome excuse to break their engagement. But he couldn't think about all that now. Not with a gunman on the loose.

Wild thoughts tumbled in his brain, vying for attention. He didn't know for sure how Leon planned to proceed with the manhunt, but Trace wanted to be a part of it. The Blake family had known too much hardship and grief. He felt an unexpected well of compassion, and knew that he had to do anything he could to help them.

The cramping in his stomach from his ulcer grew so bad that he took out the box of baking soda he kept in a desk drawer, put a spoonful of it in a glass of water and drank it.

"What was all the commotion at the doctor's office? I was busy with a customer and didn't catch it all." His father walked to the back.

"One of the Blake boys was shot." Trace gave him a quick summary of the incident.

Bill Gentry shook his head. "That family sure has had a lot of hard luck. It's been about fifteen years since they lost their oldest boy."

Trace remembered that awful time when Mr. Blake had driven like a maniac into town, his wife and four daughters in the back of the wagon. The mother had been cradling her oldest boy in her arms—much like Callie had done with Riley today—while the frightened girls crouched in the wagon bed. Callie's huge dark eyes and black hair had struck him as tragic, but so pretty. He had only been an awkward eleven-year-old at the time, but he had tried to comfort her. Today he had been struck anew with her adult beauty.

Yes, Callie's clothes were dirty and her beautiful black hair, worn in a short, practical style, was untidy, but he knew what hard work and tragedy looked like.

"The boy was only fifteen, as I recall." His dad's words reclaimed Trace's attention. "He had started to help his dad bring their steam engine to town, and the tail of his coat got caught in the cogs of the engine and pulled him into it. His arm and side were chewed up real bad."

Trace nodded as the details came back to him. "He needed more medical help than Doc could provide, so you took a new car from this showroom and took him to Rolla." Thirty-five miles north, Rolla was the nearest town with a hospital.

"The boy died on the operating table." Dad's somber

statement was accompanied by a sad shake of his head. "The next year the family's house burned down."

Trace swallowed the lump that had formed in his throat. "I remember all that, but I never had much contact with the family over the years. I believe the parents are godly people, but I sure don't see that they have much to thank God for."

Guilt stabbed at him. He had been wrapped up in his own life and pleasures, too busy working and making money to notice the brutal plight of others around him. The gnawing in his stomach worsened.

His dad picked up a cleaning rag and began to wipe fingerprints off the display car he had shown to a potential customer earlier. "Arlie and Dessie Blake are hardworking people. It's too bad their kids aren't."

The comment brought Trace up short. "What do you mean?"

Bill paused in his task and raised his head. "Those youngest two have reputations for being wild, and I've heard the boys mentioned in connection with bootlegging. It makes me wonder if the whole family is involved, or running a still of their own."

Trace remembered hearing rumors. Today's incident could mean that the boys were, indeed, mixed up in the making or selling of illegal hooch. But not Callie.

"I can't believe the whole family is involved. Especially Callie."

His dad frowned and shook his head in doubt. "I'd hate to see you get involved with that bunch. I'm afraid they can't be trusted."

Could his dad be right? Trace didn't think so. But would the man who shot Riley come back to make another attempt on Delmer's life?

He thought he could trust Callie, but today he had sensed something more to her fear. Her family appeared to need Callie's financial help as much as ever. So why had she quit her job and come home?

Callie's mind raced as she marched down the sidewalk. Fear and concern for her brother mingled with elation. *He was not engaged.* It changed nothing. Poverty had taught her not to dream. She had given up hope of ever finding love and having a home of her own.

When she got back to the doctor's office, her parents were just returning to the waiting room. Mom's eyes were red and puffy, and her salt-and-pepper hair straggled from its bun.

Dr. Randolph accompanied them. In his early sixties, the stocky man wore a solemn scowl. "See he stays in bed a few days, even if you have to tie him down. I'll stop in to check on him tomorrow afternoon."

Dad nodded. "Thanks for patching him up, Doc. We'll pay you soon as we can."

But Callie knew they wouldn't. They didn't have the money. Callie would take care of it from her dwindling savings. Should she leave and find another job? Or stay and take care of her folks? She had been on the verge of leaving, but now they needed her at home more than ever. They already had more work than they could handle, and now Riley couldn't work at the mill and had to be nursed. Guilt gnawed at Callie for bringing more trouble to them. She had to do something, and she would. But it was too big a problem to think about right now.

By the time they got Riley home, the encroaching dusk had gradually cooled the hot, muggy evening. As the sun disappeared behind a thick growth of forest foliage, her sister Clementine met them at the edge of the yard.

They got Riley inside and into the bed at the west end of the bedroom where he and Delmer slept. Blankets suspended from wires divided the long room into three sections. Mom and Dad used the east section. Callie and Clem had the middle. Callie went to fix supper while her mother stayed with Riley.

"I'm tired of eating the same old things all the time," Clem complained as she peeled potatoes. "I wish we could have something different once in a while. I'm sick of green beans. I hate snapping the things. The only thing worse is stemming gooseberries."

"Be thankful you have *anything* to eat. Many people don't. Are you going to stay in school? Or have you tried any more to find a job?"

Clem tossed her head in a gesture of disdain. "What do you care? You don't have a job."

No, she didn't. Not anymore. And Clem resented the loss of money that used to come in the mail every week.

Callie clamped her mouth shut. She couldn't share her fears with Clem, and she didn't want to fight with her and cause even more distress for the family. She stepped out the kitchen door and went to get a stick of wood for the cookstove—and a grip on her emotions. She hoped Clem would finish school, but anticipated she would quit, as all their other siblings had done.

By the time Callie went back inside, her brain had begun to churn. Maybe there *was* a way to vary their diet a little—and at the same time help some people whose circumstances were even worse than theirs.

An idea formed and grew in her mind.

After church service Sunday Callie accompanied her

best friend, Jolene Delaney, from the building. "I have an idea," she said when they arrived at the Delaney family car.

Jolene, a slender girl with long, wheat-colored hair and big hazel eyes, rolled those eyes upward. "So what else is new? You always have an idea."

Callie huffed. "Do you want to hear it or not?"

Jolene grinned and pulled the car door open. "Spit it out."

"Why don't we organize a community food swap?"

Jolene released the door handle and leaned against the fender, her expression pensive. "This is to accomplish what?"

"Well, if people from all over the area bring something they have extra of, and are tired of, we could put it all out on tables and let them choose something different to take home. It would give them more variety and a change from eating the same old things."

"Uh-huh." Jolene tapped a finger against her cheek. "And what if someone brought too much of something? What would happen to the extra?"

"Well, they could be, uh, given to someone."

"Like the ones who have hungry bellies and nothing to swap?"

Callie didn't say anything for a moment, but she didn't have to.

Jolene's face glowed. "I love the idea. I'll talk to the school board. I'm sure they'll approve of us using the school. And if we can get people who are better off to donate stuff, I can see that my neediest students get food."

Jolene taught at the Deer Creek School. Located practically across the road from Callie's home, they had both attended there through eighth grade before going to high school in town.

Suddenly Jolene's eyes glistened, and her lips trembled. She threw her arms around Callie. After a bear hug, she drew back and made a hasty swipe at her eyes. "If it works, we could branch out, swap clothes and shoes that have gotten too little for their owners, but could be used by others. We could swap all kinds of things."

Callie hugged her again. "How soon can we start? And how often should we meet?"

"I'll talk to the board president and get back to you in a day or two. If they approve it, I'll put a notice in the paper and write notes to send home with the children. Oh, Callie…" She placed a smack on Callie's cheek. "I'm so glad you came home."

Callie grinned as Jolene crawled into her dad's Model T and drove away. Then she went to pull Clem away from the Tucker boy she currently fancied and make the half-mile ride home on horseback.

Callie found her mother making chicken and dumplings. Mom looked tired, and her left hand massaged her lower back as she stirred the pot with her right. Lines etched her worn face, and loose hairs straggled from the bun coiled on the back of her head, but she smiled when Callie entered the kitchen.

"I think Riley can eat."

She rejoiced with her mother when Riley ate a small bowl of chicken and dumplings. That afternoon after Dr. Randolph stopped by and pronounced him on the mend, Callie followed the doctor to his car and presented him with the money she had taken from its hiding place. At least paying him would take one burden from her parents.

Monday evening Jolene stopped by to report that the school board had approved use of the school for their swap day, and that she had put a notice in the paper.

Wednesday morning, seeking asylum from curious eyes and the fear that dogged her, Callie tackled the mundane chore of cleaning the chicken house.

Trace's spirits lifted as he drove out of town. Business had been slow this morning, so he had decided to try again to order the wood for his display case. *And maybe see Callie again.*

He pulled in at the Blake property and parked. As he walked past the house, he spotted the realization of his thoughts coming out of the chicken house behind the backyard.

"Callie," he called over the background noise of the steam engine down the hill.

She went on back inside. Moments later she emerged carrying two wooden feeders.

He eyed the clever workmanship. "Looks like someone around here knows how to use the wood they cut."

"Dad and the boys are at the mill." She jerked a thumb in that direction and headed back inside the chicken house.

Trace winced at the abrupt dismissal. She definitely did not want to talk to him. He inhaled sharply and strode down the hill, where Arlie Blake thanked him for his intervention in getting Riley to the doctor and then gave him estimates on lumber for his project.

On the way back to his truck, Trace glanced over at the chicken house again. Knowing that Callie was in there drew him, even if he wasn't welcome.

She emerged with a shovel full of chicken droppings and carried it to the compost pile in the back. He couldn't resist following her when she returned and went back inside the building. He stepped through the doorway and looked around. "It looks like you've been very busy."

Startled, she looked up from wringing the rag she had dipped in a big bucket of water. She drew a fast breath and began to cough.

"Bleach," she explained when she could speak, waving a hand in front of her face. Her eyes moved over his dark pants and white shirt, and then at her own worn shoes and frayed dress, obviously drawing a comparison.

"You look fine," he said, meaning it.

She rolled her eyes. "I do not. I'm dirty from mucking out the home of a bunch of nasty chickens. What do you want?"

Her sharp tone made him frown. "I just wanted to tell you that I got my wood ordered, and your dad gave me an update on Riley."

"Good for you." She closed her eyes, then reopened them, her look one of contrition. "I'm sorry. I'm tired and not good company."

His heart twisted. She carried too big a load.

"You look tired. I didn't mean that in a bad way," he added quickly, hands in the air, when she went ramrod straight, eyes flashing. "I just meant that you work too hard. You could use some help."

She snorted. "The men have their hands full with the mill and farm. Mom has the house, and Clem does as little as…" She clamped her mouth shut, as if embarrassed at airing so much of her personal circumstances.

"I'll help you." The impulsive offer shocked him, but he realized he meant it.

Callie's mouth dropped. "You'll what?"

"I'll help you," he repeated, taking a rag from the pile by the door. He went to work wiping down a wall.

"You don't have to do that." Even as she protested,

Callie couldn't help but register his handsome features, long lashes and full lips that made women envious. Why did she always have to react to him like a starry-eyed kid? He only saw her as someone who needed help.

"I know I don't. Let's get this done so you can take a break and move on to whatever other chores you have waiting for you." He worked as he spoke.

"You can't do that."

He turned and studied the grim line of her mouth. "I'm able-bodied. Why can't I?"

Her hands went to her hips. "Listen, I may have drifted away from God and church attendance while I lived in Saint Louis, but I never expected others to do my work. And you're not dressed for this kind of work. You'll ruin that white shirt." She wet her rag again and tackled the roosting bars with a vengeance. The thumping of her heart drowned out the roar of the sawmill.

He turned, his arms moving a little slower as his gaze seemed to swallow her. "Speaking of jobs, did something happen to yours in the city?"

She stiffened, but kept scrubbing. "No, why?"

"I figured if you've been helping your folks financially, the fact that you're home might mean you no longer need to do that."

Callie shifted around, but didn't quite meet his eyes. "I needed to come home. That's all. Don't concern yourself about us. We're not charity cases." She spoke more sharply than she intended.

He raised his palms. "I didn't mean to get too personal or offend you, Callie. I only wish I could do more to help you. You work too hard."

"We'll be fine. Work is part of life," she pointed out. "I expect to work. So do my folks."

He stared at her another moment. Then he leaned over and brushed dirt from his pants.

"You better go home and change," she said in a milder tone. "You don't want to go back to work dirty and smelling like chicken…."

"Good point." He straightened, a hint of humor glinting from his eyes. He turned to leave, but paused. "Have you figured out why someone would want to harm your brothers?"

"That's the marshal's job." *Not yours.*

He backed away. "I'll leave you to finish."

If foolish dreams of him didn't finish her.

Chapter 3

As Trace drove back to town, Callie's image traveled with him. He hadn't realized she was so prickly, and he certainly hadn't meant to stick his foot in his mouth and offend her. He understood her pride, though. She felt self-conscious about her poor circumstances, and he had made her even more aware of them, however unintentionally. He felt bad about that.

The next morning, seated behind his desk in the rear of the showroom, he watched his brother stride across the display room toward him. When Leon neared the desk, he tossed a newspaper down onto it. "What do you know about this swap thing at the school on Saturday?"

Trace shrugged and picked up the paper. The weekly rag hit the streets each Thursday, and Trace hadn't yet seen today's copy. "Nothing."

Leon pointed at the article at the bottom of the front

page and sat in the chair next to him. "That says Jolene Delaney and Callie Blake are setting up a community food swap."

He scanned the article quickly. "Sounds like they're trying to provide some variety in diets, and maybe help some needy people at the same time. What about it?"

"Nothing, I guess. It just surprised me."

"I saw Callie yesterday, and she didn't mention it."

"Oh, you did, huh?" Thankfully, Leon didn't pursue it.

"Do you have any idea why they're doing it? We already have organizations working in the area to help people."

Trace considered. The Farm Bureau had introduced the newest farming techniques, and the Missouri Farmers Association was providing an outlet for farmers to buy farm goods and sell produce. "I suspect these gals might want to help people on a personal level, like funneling food and supplies to some of Miss Delaney's students. And Miss Blake knows enough about poverty to want to help others."

Leon nodded, seeming satisfied with his reasoning. "I'm afraid Miss Blake's brothers have gotten into more trouble than they can handle. What I'm not sure about is whether they're working for the neighbors, or if the whole family is involved."

Trace still couldn't wrap his brain around that. "Dad wondered if the family has a still of their own, but I can't believe that. I think only the boys are involved."

Leon shrugged. "I'll find out. But those gals seem pretty levelheaded, and they obviously care about others."

Trace put the paper down. "You're right. Maybe we should get some stuff from the store and add it to whatever garden produce they get. They'll know what to do with it. As Dad would say, the gesture can't hurt business." He could charge it to the company and write it off as a charitable donation.

Leon got to his feet and hitched the waist of his pants up a notch. "Always business these days. Are you going to let your experience with Beulah ruin your life, or will you look around and see that there are girls around here who aren't like her?"

Trace sighed. "I don't know. Don't rush me. I might date again, but I don't see much chance of finding another..." He couldn't speak Joanna's name.

"No, you'll never find another Joanna," Leon said gently. "But you could find someone who would truly love you, rather than use you and betray you. You've experienced the best and the worst. In my estimation, that should make you a better judge of character. Either of those two gals would be worth consideration." He jabbed a thumb toward the newspaper article, turned and walked out of the dealership.

Trace stared through the plate-glass window at his brother striding down the street, his stomach aching from stress. He got up and drank a glass of soda water. Then he went to the office in the back and stuck his head inside the doorway.

"Hey, Dad. I have some errands to run. It's almost closing time and we're not busy, so I'm going to take off early."

He went out the back door and got into his truck. Then he drove around onto Main Street and pulled up in front of Dunnigan's Grocery. Inside, he examined the neat rows of shelved goods and selected a variety of staples—flour, sugar, cornmeal, rice, crackers, coffee, baking powder, vanilla—anything that struck him as useful to a family who survived on what they could grow or hunt. When he had enough to fill a dozen sacks he toted it to the truck and loaded it in the back, questioning his motives as he worked.

For some reason he didn't quite understand, he had changed his mind about charging this to the business. It would cost him plenty, but he could cover it without hurting his savings. He felt compelled to do it.

He covered everything with the tarp he kept in the back of the truck and headed home—or rather, his parents' home. His dad had persuaded him to give up his rented house on Maple Street and move back in with them after his mother fell off the back step and broke her ankle. Since her ankle healed, he had started to move out more than once, but one parent or the other always found a reason to persuade him to stay.

Saturday morning he left the house right after breakfast, still not analyzing his motives too closely. He knew the Bible taught that people should open their hearts and hands if there were poor among them. But hovering around behind that holy mandate was a desire to help some specific people.

Deer Creek School sat back from the gravel road a couple hundred yards, centered in a two-acre plot of patchy lawn. Oak trees lined the west side of the fenced lot, and several more stood in the open front yard. Hay fields surrounded the building on three sides. To the rear of the building was a water pump, with a tin cup hanging from a pole beside it. Outhouses occupied opposite rear corners of the lot. A frame shed stood between them.

Three large steps led to the front door of the simple wooden frame school that accommodated a yearly student body of twenty to thirty children. It had been larger before families began to leave their farms to find work in the cities.

Trace sat for a moment, reluctant to take the groceries inside when he had no intention of swapping for anything. He didn't want to draw attention to himself. But the stuff wasn't going to walk inside alone.

He glanced around the yard again—and spotted a girl and boy coming around the corner of the school. They stopped behind a car to talk to someone. A closer look confirmed that they were Delmer Blake and the youngest sister, Clem.

He got out of the truck and leaned against it to wait for them to finish their conversation. When they rounded the car moments later, he pushed away from the door and locked his gaze on them, willing them to look up. When they did, he beckoned with a finger.

They approached, wary looks on their faces. Delmer was a scrawny redhead. The girl was cute enough—dark hair, big eyes and a boyish figure. She struck him as a rather sullen kid.

"Whatcha need?" Delmer wore a skeptical expression.

Trace pointed to the rear of his truck. "There's stuff back there. Could you two take it inside for me?"

The girl snorted. "It don't look to me like your back's broke. Haul your own junk inside."

Delmer's hawk eyes measured him. Then he swatted his sister's arm. "Hush, Clem. There's nothing wrong with him. He just don't want nobody knowing where the stuff came from."

"Thanks," Trace said.

Delmer shrugged. "No sweat." He climbed into the

back of the truck and lifted the tarp. Then he whistled. "Looks like quite a haul, sis. Let's get busy."

The girl hesitated, but then she took the box he handed down to her.

Callie looked up from arranging a basket of potatoes on one of the "tables" she and Jolene had formed by dragging two student desks together. Delmer and Clem entered the room, both of them carrying a grocery sack in each arm.

"Where you want this stuff?" Delmer called as they came toward Callie.

"What have you got there?"

"It's store-bought stuff," Delmer answered. He peeked inside one of the bags. "I see sugar and flour in this one." He looked in the other. "This one's rice and cornmeal."

Callie frowned, knowing they could not have provided it. "Where did it come from?"

"It was—"

"Someone asked for help toting it in." Delmer cut Clem off with a glare.

Apparently they had an anonymous donor. Good. They would take all the help they could get. Callie looked over at Jolene. "Let's set it out."

Delmer dumped his sacks on the table next to Jolene. "There's more out there."

Clem put hers down next to them and followed him back out the door. Callie and Jolene each had a bag about half-empty, the goods displayed, when they returned with another load.

"A few more trips should do it," Delmer said as he plunked down the second load.

As Clem put hers next to it, people began to gather around and select goods in trade.

Delmer and Clem continued to return with more bags of food to refill the spaces as they cleared. "You two take a sack and fill it with whatever looks more appetizing to you than the tomatoes and corn we brought," she said when they finished.

Clem's face lost some of its poutiness. "Anything we want?"

Callie nodded and extended the bag she had just emptied. "Right. When you have what you want, take it home to Mom."

The upturn of Clem's mouth flattened, but only for a moment. She turned with a swish of her skirt that fell just below her knees. Callie couldn't be too critical of Clem's bobbed hair, because she had cut her own almost as short when she…

She broke off the thought, determined to concentrate on the present. She watched Delmer and Clem select what they wanted, and then leave to take it home.

Several minutes later Callie looked up and saw Trace Gentry enter the school and glance around. Her heart did a strange little thump as she watched him amble to a table and inspect it. Which was stupid. The man was an impossible dream—not that she was dreaming.

Jolene sidled up next to her. "What's he doing here? He sure isn't looking for food."

"More like bringing food," Callie whispered, turning slightly to face away from him.

Jolene glanced sideways at the table. "You think he sent this stuff?"

"I have a sneaking suspicion it was him."

Callie knew Trace had a soft heart, so she had no trouble believing he would do such a thing. She may have been only seven years old when her oldest brother had been mortally injured, but that horrible day was forever etched in her memory. She had crept into a corner of the car dealership to cry while Trace's dad and her parents loaded Everett into a car from the showroom and set out for the hospital in Rolla. Eleven-year-old Trace had sat down beside her and held her hand. When he asked if she was hungry, she had nodded that she was. He had left and returned minutes later with a sandwich and a candy bar, an unheard-of treat for her.

That kind act accounted for the strange twinges that had bothered her stomach every time she heard his name over the years. But what was causing her to turn giddy and goose-bumpy now?

As if summoned, Trace turned and came toward them through the growing number of people milling about the room.

"How can we help you?" Jolene asked as he approached.

"I don't need anything," he said easily. "I'm just interested in the community work you two are doing here and wanted to see how it's going." His eyes passed over Jolene's beautiful coil of wheat-colored hair, to her soft gray skirt and white blouse tucked into the waist of it, all neat and pristine.

Then he turned his gaze on to Callie. The dowdiness she always felt next to her dear friend intensified. She knew her own plain cotton dress, worn thin in places, and heavy work shoes paled in comparison.

"I'm pleased with the turnout." Jolene glanced around at the mingling crowd that consisted mostly of women.

"It appears successful to me," Trace said. "Do you plan to do this again?"

Jolene shrugged. "That decision depends on today's response." She looked at Callie. "What's your feeling at this point?"

Callie had been perfectly content to let Jolene carry the conversation. She cleared her throat. "I think it's successful enough to continue."

Jolene smiled at Trace. "There's your answer. I'll get a notice to the paper Monday."

Trace focused on Callie. "How about if I put a poster in the window of the dealership advertising it?"

An automatic beam crossed her face. Their gazes caught, and Callie found herself being drawn into the depths of his deep blue eyes. She forced herself to look away. "That would be great. You're in a location where people walk past you all the time."

"Good luck." Trace spoke over his shoulder as he walked away. Callie had to force her attention back to business.

Jolene practically bubbled as she made sure certain people got supplies she knew they needed. "This is going so well, why don't we go ahead and expand?" she suggested after sending a couple of women away with a bag of staples.

Callie eyed her friend. "That sounds good. What kind of things do you want to include?"

Jolene considered for a moment. "I'm not sure what people want to exchange, possibly tools, or even furniture. If we announce that other things are welcome, it might be interesting to see what people bring."

Callie agreed. "Put it in the newspaper that way, and

we'll see what happens." She licked her dry lips. "I'm thirsty. How about you?"

Jolene nodded. "I could use a drink."

"I'll go draw some water and bring you a cup."

"I'll stay in here and keep an eye on things."

As she rounded the building, she spotted Clem and Delmer at the edge of the schoolyard. They had made good time going home and back. She stopped to watch them circle a couple of cars and approach a neighbor. They spoke for a minute. Then Delmer pulled a piece of paper and pencil from his pocket and wrote something down.

They moved on across the yard to another neighbor and did the same. As they circulated, Callie's stomach knotted. She had suspected the boys of involvement in bootlegging, but she had thought—hoped—that Riley's being shot would scare them into quitting. Instead, it looked like Clem had taken Riley's place. Whether Delmer had recruited her, or she had pressured him into it, Callie had no idea.

Lord, please stop them. Please show me what to do.

Movement farther over caught her eye. Trace Gentry had his sights trained on her younger siblings. He must know—or at least suspect—what they were doing.

A black car drove slowly up the road. As it passed the school, fear shot through Callie. She stared at the driver, whose face wasn't clearly visible. But he reminded her of the shooter. When the car went on past, she exhaled a long slow breath and decided she must be growing paranoid, seeing danger in everything. She started toward the front steps.

When she saw the car coming back, she came to an abrupt stop and watched it pull into the schoolyard and stop next to the fence. The driver got out and walked along the perimeter of the yard. He wore black pants and shirt, with a black hat pulled down over his eyes. As he walked, he glanced around.

No longer uncertain, Callie's heart leaped to her throat. She looked around in panic. Where had Clem and Delmer gone?

Chapter 4

Trace started to leave, but hesitated when he saw Callie Blake come around the corner of the school building with a cup in her hands and come to a stop. Then he saw her go rigid and almost drop the cup. He followed her line of vision and shared her reaction. A man was walking among the cars. The brim of his hat hid his eyes, but his body language said he was on the hunt.

In a flash Trace understood. This man matched the description of the one who had shot Riley. He had to be looking for Delmer—who could identify him.

Trace backed off the running board and raised his hand in a signal to catch the man's attention, walking at a fast clip toward him. In his peripheral vision he saw Callie take advantage of the distraction, gather her wits and dash across the front of the building. She ducked down behind a car, worked her way around it and made a running beeline for her brother and sister at the edge of the yard.

The man halted and aimed a dark glare across the yard at Trace. Then he spun and headed back toward his car. Trace glanced over to see that Callie had reached her siblings and was talking heatedly to them. For a second it appeared that Delmer would take off after the man, but Callie's grip on his arm prevented such a foolhardy action. The three of them ducked down behind a car.

Trace started to pursue the man, but it was too late. He had reached his car and jumped inside. As he started the motor, Trace spun and ran back to his truck. By the time he got it started, the car had backed out into the road and taken off. He put the truck in gear and followed.

He drove as fast as he could, but lost sight of the car about a half mile from town. Scanning the countryside either side of him, he considered that it must have turned off onto a side road. He smacked the steering wheel in frustration. But then he considered the fact that the man carried a gun, and decided to drive on into town. He reported what he had seen to Leon and headed back to his truck. When he got behind the wheel, he bowed his head.

Lord, the Blake family has always needed Your help, but they especially need it right now. Please watch over them and protect them.

Trace hoped God would listen to his plea. After Joanna's death he had failed to pray as he ought. In his grief and loneliness he had strayed from God and made some very wrong decisions.

Please forgive me, Father.

He raised his head and started the engine. When he reached the school, there were only four cars left in the yard. He parked and went inside, but didn't see Delmer and Clem.

Jolene and Callie were helping a woman fill a sack. Elderly with no family left, Mrs. Brown could undoubtedly use the extra food.

Callie came around the table to meet him, and he said, "Let's go outside where we can talk."

They made their way outside and stood beside his truck in the schoolyard. "Where are your brother and sister?"

"I sent them home and told them to stay there." Her eyes searched his face. "Did you catch him?"

He shook his head. "No, I lost him just this side of town. I went on to the jail and told Leon about him."

"What did you tell him?" Her speech came out uneven and tremulous.

Trace studied her expression. She tried to hide her fear, but the worry in her eyes gave her away. "I told him I thought Riley's shooter had returned. Am I mistaken?"

Her hands clenched, and her breathing sounded shallow. Finally she nodded.

Frustration coursed through him. He had to make her open up to him. "That man is looking for two things. He wants to know if Riley's dead. And he wants to silence Delmer because he's a witness. Is that all?"

When she still didn't speak, he studied her white face. "Callie, you have to tell me why you're so afraid. What is that man after?" His tone bordered on anger. Couldn't she see the danger she was putting her family in if she knew something that would help stop a gunman and didn't tell it?

She swallowed and gnawed at her lip. A film came over her eyes, squeezing his heart. He stared into those shiny orbs and wished he could wrap her in his arms and comfort her.

She gulped and visibly fought back the tears. "It should have been me," she said, the words so low and strained he could hardly hear them. She slumped back against the truck.

He took a step nearer, then tamped down on the impulse to reach for her. "What do you mean?"

Callie stared at him, her chin quivering. "I saw something I shouldn't have. That's why I came home. I ran."

His mind raced ahead as the puzzle started to fall into place. "Tell me about it," he urged, no longer angry.

Her breathing pattern changed, quickened, and a look of resignation came over her face. She crossed her arms and tugged at the sleeve of her dress. Then she took a deep breath and pulled herself upright. "As you know, when I was eighteen I went to work in Saint Louis. My parents were having a real hard time, and I couldn't find work here."

"You sent them money," he prompted when her words trailed to a halt.

She nodded. "I sent them everything I had left after expenses." She paused, and then produced a wobbly smile. "But I wanted to buy a car."

"A car, huh?" What irony that she dreamed of the very thing he took for granted.

"I got a second job so I could save for one."

"What kind of work did you do?"

"When I first got to the city, a cousin helped me find a room in a boardinghouse. Right after I moved in, I found out that the woman who ran it needed a maid. I applied, and she hired me. I worked for two years before I got the other job." She ran her tongue over her lips.

"A night job?"

She nodded. "Styles had changed. Girls wore different clothes and hairstyles. I cut my hair shorter and got some boy's clothes from a thrift center. Then I went to the hotel a few blocks from the boardinghouse where I had seen a sign advertising for a bellhop. I applied, using the name Cal, and told them I wanted to work nights and weekends. They hired me."

Trace had no trouble visualizing a twenty-year-old Callie posing as a boy. Slender and dark haired, and with her country background, she would not only have looked like a boy, but she would have worked like one.

"Everything went fine," she continued, as if she couldn't tell it fast enough now that she had started. "I would work all day at the boardinghouse, get something to eat and take a bag of boy clothes down the street to a gas station with a restroom. I would go in there and change. Then, at the hotel, I would change again, into the uniform the hotel provided."

She paused, and her voice softened with regret. "I wanted a car so much that, instead of asking God for one and trusting Him to show me how to get it, I set out to get it on my own."

"What happened?" he asked when she stopped, her hands clenched together in a knot.

It was several seconds before she swallowed and continued. "One night I took a couple and their luggage up to the third floor. They were in a hurry to leave and asked me to put their bags away and call a cab for them. They went back downstairs while I was making the call."

"So you were alone."

She nodded. "When I got done, I left the room. As I rounded a corner to the stairs, I saw two men at the end of the hall. They were arguing, and suddenly one of them pulled out a gun and shot the other one."

The final piece clicked into place. "Did he see you?"

Her face went even whiter. "He looked up just as I got to the corner of the hall and saw me. I turned and ran down the stairs. I heard him coming after me. Fortunately, I was faster than him."

"So you packed up and left town," he finished for her. He understood so much now. Scared, she had run home, the only haven she knew. Now that she had been found, she felt responsible for putting her brothers in danger, yet she couldn't run again and abandon them. "You need to stay hidden as much as possible."

"I won't do anything foolish," she promised in an unsteady voice. "But I have to help Mom and Dad all I can now that I don't have a job. Right now I need to get home and be sure Riley and Delmer are all right. Keeping them out of sight won't be easy."

"I know they have to work, but surely they'll be careful if you explain it to them. I'll go back to town now and tell Leon what you just told me."

As he started to walk away, Callie remembered something else. "I, uh…if you should happen to know who sent those groceries that Delmer and Clem carried in, would you tell him…or her…that Jolene and I thank them on behalf of the people who received them?"

He hesitated, his eyes staring over her head and beyond. She took that as confirmation that she had guessed right.

"I'm sure you girls found places where they would help most," he said, clearly uncomfortable.

"Yes, we did," she assured him. "Jolene knows which

students would benefit the most. She made sure that those of them who showed up got extra stuff."

He ran a hand over his face. "Good. You have generous hearts. I wish you continued success in this."

Callie watched him drive away. Then she went back inside and helped Jolene push the desks back into place and tidy the room.

When they finished and Jolene drove away, Callie walked the short distance home, her mind in a whirl. She had a gangster after her. Trace was free, but his life was still a world away from hers. It was foolish to waste time dreaming about him.

Trace drove home, oblivious to the blur of brown fields and dust-filled air. His thoughts bounced from Callie Blake, to her brother, to what she had told him. The gunman had mistaken Riley for her. Which meant she and her brothers were all in danger.

He drove straight to the jail. Seated behind a small table he used as a desk, Leon looked up from studying a paper. "What's wrong?"

Trace dropped onto the chair by the door. "I'm worried about the Blake family. That gunman was looking for Callie and mistook Riley for her." He repeated Callie's story.

Leon shook his head. "She could be right, but if she can't positively identify him I can't rule out the possibility that someone is trying to cut in on the local bootlegging business."

Trace sighed in frustration. "She's really scared, and if she's right they're still in danger. I think he'll hang around to make sure Cal's dead."

"And to shoot the other brother," Leon added.

Trace raised another point. "From what Callie said, I don't think the man saw her, but there's always a chance he did. If he finds out Riley's alive, he'll try again."

Leon rubbed a hand back and forth over his chin. "I'll call a friend in Saint Louis law enforcement and see if he can connect Callie's story to any killing up there. While he's at it, I'll also ask if he can put out the word up there that Cal—" he stressed the name "—died. I can't do that down here, but we can do our best to convince the family to keep the boys out of sight, maybe even say the younger boy got so scared he left town."

Trace nodded. "It can't hurt."

Leon eyed him carefully. "You're the perfect person to keep an eye on them. Hate to run out on you, but I have a meeting. I'll get to a phone while I'm out." He picked up his hat and left.

Trace stopped at the diner for a sandwich. Then he spent the afternoon at the business. His dad no longer worked every day, so a slow day like this one was a good opportunity to catch up on book work and miscellaneous chores. He stared at the back wall and mentally planned the display case he wanted back there.

Three years ago the Ford Agency building had been built down the street. It gave them some stiff competition, but they had held their own. Sales had fallen off this past year, though. He needed to turn that around, run some kind of special. But nothing came to him.

When Clem and Delmer didn't show up for supper, Callie worried about them. The look on her mother's face told her that those worries were shared. She didn't argue when Mom suggested they go to bed early.

Lord, watch over Clem and Delmer, she prayed silently

as she lay there unable to sleep. *They've been taught to live by Your word, but they seem to have turned their backs on You. Please work in their lives. Show me if there's something I can do.*

Callie didn't know how long she had slept when sounds woke her. The bedroom door eased open, and then she heard sounds of Clem getting ready for bed. Not wanting to wake their parents—if they were sleeping—Callie kept silent.

At breakfast the next morning, Clem and Delmer ate quickly and darted outside to do the chores they should have done earlier.

Mom drew a deep breath. "I hope they aren't involved with the wrong people."

Callie did, too, but her gut tightened. "I'll do the dishes. You go on and get ready for church. I'll catch up."

Mom didn't argue, which Callie took as an indication of her worried state.

"Callie."

Callie looked up from wiping the table minutes later. Her mother stood in the doorway. She came to the table and held out two five-dollar bills. "Take this back, dear. It was hard enough taking money from you when you had a job. Don't give me what you must have struggled to save." Her voice quavered.

Callie stepped back, palms up and shaking her head in denial. "I don't know what you're talking about."

Mom's face drew into a frown, gauging Callie's sincerity. "You sure?"

"Absolutely."

Mom turned her hand over and stared at the money. "I found this in my purse. I know it wasn't there the last time I had it open."

A look of possible understanding flashed across her face, and a hand went over her mouth. "Do you think Clem or Delmer put it there?"

Callie shrugged. "I don't know."

"But where would they get it?" She spoke more to herself than Callie.

Callie had an idea, but she didn't want to voice it. "You'll have to ask them."

As they rode in the wagon, Callie smoothed the skirt of her blue gingham dress and tried not to worry about Riley. He had insisted he was strong and they should all go to church. She wished for the umpteenth time that her parents could afford a car. The possibility of buying one of her own moved farther beyond her reach every time she had to dip into her little savings.

A cool breeze came up. The leaves had not started changing colors yet, but would within a week or two. Right now the countryside was still beautiful with its rolling tree-covered hills and splashes of lush greenery. Farm ponds and parched hay fields dotted the landscape. The serenity of the familiar scenes normally would have brought a sense of calmness to Callie and eased the turmoil inside her. But today nothing soothed her troubled spirit.

While in Saint Louis she had come to rely on her own strengths, while growing lax and ceasing to consult God about her decisions. The weekend-evening job had not left time for regular church attendance. Over time she had stopped going altogether. Since coming home, she had begun attending again.

It only took fifteen minutes to drive to the small frame church about a mile from the house. It had stood in that grove for over twenty years, but Dad, Riley and Delmer

had cut the lumber and built the porch across the front
of it only three years ago.

Although it felt good to be back in church, Callie continued to worry as she and Jolene shared a hymnbook.
After the song service, the pastor read from the Book
of Ruth.

"A lot of people are having a real hard time now. We
need to take a lesson from Naomi. She never lost sight
of the fact that God is capable and faithful. Remember
that Naomi's God is also your God. Let's be about our
work and not worry about tomorrow. The scripture says
tomorrow will worry about its own things, sufficient for
the day is its own trouble."

Callie drew a deep breath. Constant worry wore her
down. Could she really keep from it, with so little money
to buy what they needed? They had chickens, raised a
big garden and had some fruit trees. This fall they would
butcher a pig, and Dad and the boys hunted wild game.
They didn't always eat well, but they didn't go hungry
like they had back when Mom and Dad had seven small
kids to feed. But the fear of going hungry always lurked
in the back of Callie's mind.

Her sisters Cora and Celia now lived in neighbor-
ing small towns with their husbands. They just got by,
but having them on their own meant two less mouths to
feed here. Riley's desire to earn some extra money didn't
shock Callie, but his apparent involvement in bootlegging did. She expected better judgment from him. His
getting shot was her fault, but the risk of being arrested
for peddling hooch was his.

"Fear reveals our wish to protect the things in life that
are important to us, rather than fully entrusting them to
God's control and care. When we allow fear to take over,

it cripples us emotionally and saps us spiritually. A fearful spirit makes us vulnerable to the enemy, who tempts us to compromise biblical teachings and take matters into our own hands."

The biting truth of his words sank deep inside Callie. Fear had caused her to quit her job and flee home. Now fear had immobilized her. She didn't know what to do.

I want to trust You to take care of us, Lord. Please give me courage and help me not to worry so much. When I am afraid, I will trust in Thee, she quoted silently.

After the benediction Pastor Denlow announced that the community swap meet would be held again the coming Saturday, and that items in addition to food would be welcome.

"I've gotten the word out. Can you get there early to set up?" Jolene asked before they parted outside the door.

"Sure."

Jolene tipped her head, eyes narrowed. "It'll be interesting to see who shows up. And if there are any more anonymous donations."

"Let's go, Jolene," her ten-year-old sister, Irene, begged. "I'm hungry."

Jolene rolled her eyes. "You're always hungry. Get in the car. I'll be there in a minute."

She turned back to Callie. "Mother wasn't feeling well this morning, and Dad stayed home to take care of her. I need to check on him."

A twinge of concern ate at Callie as she watched Jolene follow her little black-haired sister to their car. Isabelle Delaney had been sick a long time after Irene's birth ten years ago. Then she seemed to get better. But she never fully regained her strength and struggled to take care of her husband and two daughters. Jolene had taken over more and more responsibilities around the home and, over time, had become the child's mother figure.

After dinner Callie took Riley a bowl of soup and spooned it to him. When he finished, he lay back, exhausted, and directed a troubled gaze up at her.

"So sorry, Callie. I never shoulda let the guys talk me into that bootlegging mess. I don't know what happened to make you come home…don't need to know." He paused to get his breath. "I just wanted to help…take some of the burden you been carrying. They made it sound like easy money…and they promised that no one would get hurt. Sorry." His eyes closed.

Seeing that he had fallen asleep, Callie took the bowl back to the kitchen. Guilt choked her. Riley thought someone connected to his bootlegging activities had shot him.

Monday morning Riley joined them for breakfast, his eyes brighter. When they finished eating, he came up behind Callie as she put the leftover biscuits in the warming oven. He tapped her on the nose with an index finger and snatched a biscuit.

Callie eyed her brother. "You sit back down and eat that. Let your body heal."

"Yes, ma'am." He winked. Then his expression turned serious. "I'm sorry you're upset with me and Delmer."

She took a deep breath and poured hot water into the dishpan. "I'm not upset with you. Well, maybe a little. I understand that you wanted to help the folks, but I think you know now that it wasn't a good way to do it."

He nodded. "I guess I let worry take over. I knew better, but I didn't listen and really messed up. Now I'm worried about Delmer."

Callie started to say, "And Clem," but didn't. Riley

didn't need any more concerns right now. "I guess we both need to listen to God more."

Riley ignored the reference to God. "Callie, don't you ever want to stop taking care of the family and have a life of your own?"

Of course I do. "I don't see that in my future."

"You should. You aren't responsible for anyone but yourself."

I feel like I am. "I won't abandon Mom and Dad, or the rest of you." Even for a dream of love, or for someone like Trace.

Chapter 5

Trace sat in the chair in Carl's barbershop, getting his hair cut. "What does Leon think happened with that Blake boy? Does he know yet who shot him?"

Trace started to shake his head, but didn't when a picture of the barber's scissors catching him in the ear flashed in his mind. "I don't know, but I'm sure he's working on it."

"There's been a lot of talk. Some people think those Blake boys are feuding with their neighbors."

"It wasn't anyone from around here. The younger boy and his sister got a look at the guy." He didn't mention seeing the man at the school.

Carl paused, scissors and comb suspended. "You mean the older sister, Callie, right?"

Trace dipped his head. "She saw him, but she was over beside the house, and she doesn't think he saw her."

Carl tapped the comb against Trace's head, then began to snip again. "Now there's a gal who would be a nice catch for someone. But everybody knows that family doesn't amount to much. I hear those youngest two are pretty wild. Maybe she's no different."

Trace swallowed his irritation. "She can't be blamed for what members of her family do. She's a hard worker and contributes to her family and the community. She and her girlfriend want to share what they have."

"That's better than Beulah…oops, sorry. Didn't mean to get so personal."

Trace sighed. News of his broken engagement had gotten around. "No problem."

When Carl finished his haircut, Trace got into his truck and headed to the Blakes' place to get his lumber. Business had been brisk Monday. He and his dad had taken delivery of four new Independence model cars that Chevrolet had built in response to Ford's successful Model A. They had also shown cars to several potential customers and sold one. In contrast, today was so slow that Trace had decided to get a haircut and go get his lumber while his dad took care of the business.

He pulled in at the Blake home and got out of the truck. He didn't see anyone around, but could hear the saw ripping wood down at the mill. Mrs. Blake answered his knock on the door.

"Hello, Mrs. Blake. Is Riley doing okay?"

She wiped her hands on her bibbed apron. "He's getting around more each day." She stepped back in a manner that invited him inside the house.

He went up the two wooden steps and entered a square living room. A stove and wood box occupied much of the east side of the room. Riley sat in the only comfortable chair. He looked pale and listless, but he gripped the arms of the chair and looked up. On a shelf behind him a pendulum worked back and forth in a wooden clock.

"Hi, Mr. Gentry."

"Name's Trace." He walked over and extended a hand.

Riley shook it and leaned back while his mother hovered near the chair. "Okay, Trace. They say you took me to the doctor. Thanks. What can we do for you?"

"I wanted to check and be sure you're all right." He stared at the young man and was startled at how much he and Callie looked alike. He hadn't really noticed such a strong resemblance before. Of course, Callie's story made him look for it.

"I'm getting stronger. I'll be back to work soon."

"Not too soon," Mrs. Blake cautioned.

"Good. Do you have any idea who shot you?" He felt certain that Callie had not told them her story. But he wanted to gauge Riley's manner when asked about it.

Riley's head rotated back and forth slowly. "I wish I did. I never saw that guy before. Has the marshal found out anything?"

"Nothing very helpful. He's checking with some friends in other police departments, seeing if they make any connections. Is your brother staying out of sight?"

Riley frowned. "I don't know. He's working with Dad at the mill. They said something about needing to quit early and go to town to get a new belt for the tractor."

Trace tried to sound casual. "Leon says he should keep low. He's going to put out the word that Delmer left town so the man will hopefully stop looking for him. Is Callie around?"

Riley gave him a speculative look. "She was around earlier."

"She went to the pond," Mrs. Blake volunteered. "She said she wanted something different for supper."

So she had gone fishing. "Where is the pond?"

Riley jerked a thumb toward the west wall. "Cross that field out there. It's down in the next pasture."

Trace gave Mrs. Blake another look. "I'd like to talk to her a minute. Do you mind if I go find her after I pick up the materials I ordered?"

"That'd be fine." She left the room through a door at the back of the living room that he figured must lead to a bedroom. He had trouble comprehending a family the size of theirs living in three rooms.

"You take care and stay out of sight for a while," he cautioned Riley. "Leon said he's keeping an eye on this place."

Riley nodded. "We've seen him drive by several times."

Trace exited the house and drove his truck down next to the sawdust pile where Mr. Blake and Delmer were sawing logs. Behind them was a barn and fenced lot. Back of the barn hogs snorted and rooted in a pen.

"Over here." Arlie Blake pointed at a pile of lumber.

Trace pulled alongside it and got out.

He and Delmer loaded the lumber and Trace paid for it. "Is it okay if I leave the truck here while I stop by and speak to Callie?"

Mr. Blake's eyes took on a speculative gleam. "It's not in the way. Go ahead. I take it you know where to find her?"

Trace nodded in the direction of the pond.

"Run on. Take your time."

Trace hiked across the field and crossed a fence. Dusty air drifted over tall grass that had parched and turned brown. A bit farther he spotted the pond. As he reached the grove of trees at one side of it, the air smelled a little cleaner.

From the tree line he spotted Callie. Curious, he paused next to a big oak and drank in the sight of her. With her back to him, she stood poised at the edge of the pond, staring intently at the water. She wore what looked like a brother's overalls, the pant legs rolled up to her knees, and held something in her hand. When she raised her arms, he recognized a slingshot.

Trace watched, transfixed, as Callie inserted a stone in the pocket, pulled the rubber strips back and took careful aim. Then she released the missile. It plunked right between the two eyes bulging up from the water. The body of a frog instantly flattened on the surface, knocked unconscious.

In a flash Callie grabbed the tree branch lying near her feet and waded into the edge of the water. Then she reached out and raked the frog in with the stick. She pulled it up with a hand and carried it over to the stump where a big bucket sat.

She picked up a string attached to the bail of the big bucket. Several frogs dangled from it. She attached the new catch and dropped them all back into the bucket with a splash. Turning slightly, she spotted him and jumped in surprise.

He moved toward her. "I didn't mean to startle you."

"I had no idea anyone was near," she said breathlessly, her body language telling him that he made her nervous. She kicked the tree branch away from her bare feet. "What in the world are you doing out here?"

He eyed the bucket of frogs. "Being impressed by some incredible marksmanship."

She flushed slightly.

"I didn't mean to make you uncomfortable," he apologized, walking closer. The freckles across her nose drew his attention. Pink tinged her cheeks when their eyes met. He had to force his gaze away before he did something stupid, like grab her and kiss her. What in the world was he thinking?

Callie pulled a rag from her pocket and wiped her hands. "What's on your mind?"

"I came to check on you and your brothers. I'm glad to see that Riley is improving."

Her eyes narrowed. "Because you think that man will try again to shoot Delmer."

He nodded. "Leon says all three of you should stay out of sight. I agree."

"But we have to work," she protested.

His muscles tensed. He couldn't admit to her, or even to himself, that she was becoming important to him. Way too important. He got a grip on his emotions and repeated the warning he had given Riley. "I understand, but your safety is important, too."

Her face had gone pale when he spoke of the gunman. He nodded toward the big stump next to her frog bucket. "Let's sit down."

She tugged at the strap of her overalls and scooted onto the stump.

He sat next to her. "Leon says if you can't positively identify the man, he still has to consider the possibility that someone is trying to move in on the local bootlegging. He's going to contact some friends in Saint Louis. He hopes if they put out the word that Cal—" he put emphasis on the name "—died and Delmer left town that whoever is after them will figure he's done his job and go away."

Callie nodded, her legs swinging against the stump. Her face looked troubled. "No, I can't swear it's him, but I know inside me that it is."

"If it's him, Leon will find out. If it's not, there's something else that bothers me. Gangsters and bootleggers usually work in pairs. That guy was alone. If he's tied to bootlegging, I'm guessing he has a contact in the area."

She gnawed on her lip. "He shoots people, so he might be working for one of the city gangsters. I guess he could have come looking for me and just happened to find what looks like a fresh source of liquor for his boss."

"That's good thinking."

He watched her throat work as she swallowed. Her lips tantalized him. "Delmer can work at the mill without being seen from the road. Riley's still inside the house most of the time."

Searching for a way to keep an eye on her, Trace had an idea. "How about if I hang around Saturday morning and help you and Jolene with your community swap meet?"

He couldn't read her thoughts, but he sensed her heightened tension. "I'd find ways to occupy myself, and help you. Don't you trust me?"

She shifted her position on the stump and glanced away, clearly uncomfortable. "I trust you," she said at last.

Trace rolled his shoulders. "You're a smart lady."

She looked down at her overalls and snickered. "Some lady I am. More like a hillbilly tomboy."

With that she swung her legs around and hopped off the stump. She ran over to the grassy area where a pair of shoes rested and sat down.

"Are you done frog hunting?" he asked as she put them on.

She didn't look up. "Yep."

He slid off the stump and reached for the bail of her frog bucket. "I'll carry this for…"

As he picked up the heavier than expected bucket, his foot plunged into the murky pond water. He yelped.

Now she did look up. And a beautiful smile lit her face.

He extended a hand for an assist. But she ignored it. And laughed.

Callie hacked at the frogs as she cleaned them, giddiness making her reckless. The look on Trace's face when he slipped into the water and she laughed at him had been priceless. Then he had walked beside her, his shoe squishing, and deliberately sloshed water on her all the way back to the house.

A vision of his features lived in her mind as the frog legs sizzled in the skillet. High cheekbones, a square jaw, fathomless blue eyes with little creases at the corners, dark lashes. Everything she could want in a man—if she were free to dream of one.

Trace had been a leader in high school, an athlete, and one of the few boys with a car of his own. Relaxed and carefree, he had made others feel at ease and important around him. Except for Callie. She had been jealous of the girls who flirted with him so easily, and of the pretty clothes they wore. Even if she had not been four years younger, she would never have been comfortable, or welcome, in his social world.

She didn't understand Trace's interest in her family. She had no doubt, however, that his concern was for the entire family and their safety, not her specifically. Even if she were accustomed to the attention of men, a man like him would never be seriously interested in an invisible nobody like her.

Lord, help me stop mooning over what can never be.

After supper Clem and Delmer darted out the door.

"That's getting to be a habit," Dad growled at Mom. "They're dodging chores, figuring Callie will do 'em now she's home. The Bible says them that don't work don't eat. They better learn that." He slapped a palm on the table and got up.

"It's all right," Callie said as he grabbed his hat. Actually, it wasn't all right. But she didn't know how much they suspected about the suspicious activities of their youngest children. And they had enough to deal with—working their fingers to the bone just to survive, and worrying about Riley, who had eaten better tonight.

"I'll be back to work soon." Riley aimed a grim expression across the table "As soon as I do, I'll drag Delmer right along with me."

And I'll let Clem know that I won't be doing her chores any longer.

Callie was torn. If she worked at the mill to keep Riley from doing too much, that would leave her mother with too much work. But she had to find a way to make some money.

Dad faced Riley from the doorway. "You take all the time you need. I'll be explaining things to Delmer soon as I catch up with him." He stalked out, slamming the door behind him.

Chapter 6

"You about ready?"

"I'll be along in a few minutes."

Trace watched his dad leave. He had entered the family business partly because of Leon's abdication. His dad had been none too pleased when his brother had chosen to enforce the law rather than sell cars. But Trace truly liked being around vehicles and learning about engines.

Last night he had run into Jolene Delaney at the ice cream shop and surprised himself again by offering to take her place Saturday morning if she needed to stay home with her ill mother. Jolene had insisted that she would be there, but had accepted his offer to arrive early and help Callie set up.

Callie's image returned. He pictured her: always working, her black hair pushed back, her manner gentle and caring. She had known poverty but had not let it sour her on life. Instead, she found ways—like this community swap meet—to help others. He swiped at his mouth with a napkin and got up to go to work. But he couldn't wipe away the image.

Saturday morning Callie fumed as she hitched the horses to the loaded buckboard. The evening before, she had walked to town and found Clem and Delmer hanging out with the Lonigan boys, Troy and Chuckie. Their family lived a rough and tumble existence and would see running a still as a good business. From what she knew of the Lonigans, they would take delight in outsmarting the law.

Deeply troubled that her siblings were forsaking God's teachings and harming the reputation of their family, she had confronted them. Delmer had admitted putting the money in Mom's purse and where he got it. He had seemed contrite, but had not promised to change. Clem had stalked away in anger.

Callie finished hitching the team and climbed up onto the seat of the buckboard. Even though she had been shy because of her impoverished background and lack of social skills as a girl, she had shared the dreams of most of her friends and classmates—having a handsome man fall in love with her, marrying him and having a family of her own. Apparently God's plan for her life didn't fit those early dreams.

So why did thoughts of Trace Gentry still make her brain turn to sawdust?

When Callie drove the buckboard into the schoolyard, she found Trace waiting next to his truck. He came to meet her as she pulled to a stop next to the building.

"What's all this?" He peered over the side of the wagon bed.

She looped the reins around the whip handle anchored at the end of the seat. "Several people stopped by this week and dropped off things they wanted to donate. Even though it's such a short distance, I couldn't carry it all."

He whistled. "I should say not. It looks like you've got a lot more than food there."

When she started to climb down, he gave her an assist. Then he took a load of clothes from the wagon. "Lead the way."

Callie fought to control the runaway pace of her heart as she grabbed a sack of shoes and went to open the door with the key Jolene had given her earlier in the week.

They scooted desks around and arranged the room to display items. When that was done, Callie looked around, hands on hips, and frowned.

"What's the matter?"

She did a little nose wrinkle. "We're okay for the food, but how can we arrange the rest of this stuff? We don't have any racks to hang the clothes on, and it'll be chaos if people start rummaging through piles on the floor."

Trace considered a moment. "How about I run and get some sawhorses and boards. It won't be as good as racks, but we can make a long table across that wall." He pointed to the left of the front door. "You can at least fold things and keep them off the floor."

She nodded. "That's a good idea. Thanks."

"I'll be back soon."

A few minutes later Trace entered with a pair of sawhorses and positioned them next to the wall. Two men followed with a stack of boards. Within minutes they fashioned a crude table.

"Thanks, guys," Trace said as the men left. Then he held out his arms for the armload of clothing Callie had gathered.

She grinned. "Let's put male stuff at one end of the table and female at the other."

"Got it." His smile was pure charm.

He takes orders well. Callie's mouth twitched as she watched him walk away, her heart galloping. She didn't understand why he had gotten involved, but she appreciated his help. And him. She picked up another load and followed him.

"I told Leon about what you saw in that hotel," Trace said quietly as they worked. "He got back to me the next day and said the police captain in Saint Louis he talked to matched your story and the date to a killing in their files. The captain put some pictures in the mail for you to look at and see if you can identify the killer you saw. They should be here any time."

A band of fear squeezed her heart. "I have to identify him?"

"If you can."

She swallowed and drew a deep breath. "I'll try."

Jolene came rushing through the door. "Sorry I'm so late," she apologized breathlessly. She glanced around the room. "But it looks like you have everything under control."

A woman walked up and handed Callie a sack of green beans. "Thank you, Mrs. Dooley."

The woman nodded and moved on. Callie placed the bag on the produce table. People continued to arrive. Last week's attendance had already been surpassed, and it was only eight o'clock. Callie started to comment on that fact, but Jolene's solemn expression kept her from it. "How's your mother?"

Jolene's mouth tightened, and she shook her head. Her eyes glistened. "Not good."

Isabelle Delaney's health had seemed to deteriorate more rapidly this past year. Callie wrapped her arms around her friend's shoulder. "Is she worse?"

Jolene's head bobbed. "She stays in bed most of the time. Dad looks after her while Irene and I are at school. We do as much as we can after we get home."

Callie stroked Jolene's hair. "You should be home now."

Jolene shook her head and withdrew from Callie's arms. "I can't let Irene stay in the house all the time. She needs to be around other children. And Dad insists we keep our lives as normal as possible as…as long as we can." Her choked voice broke Callie's heart.

"You know I welcome your help, but I'll look after things any time you need to stay home. Okay?"

Jolene nodded.

"Hello, Miss Delaney." Trace held out a hand. "It's nice to see you again."

Jolene gave him a wan smile. "You're a welcome pair of hands, Trace. Callie and I appreciate it."

"Pleased to help. I couldn't help but overhear your conversation. I hope your mother gets to feeling better."

"Me, too." Jolene swallowed and blinked back tears.

Callie's attention was drawn to the doorway as Marshal Leon Gentry came through it and headed toward them.

"Glad to find both you girls here. Miss Jolene, I hope your mother is better."

Jolene shrugged. "She needs a lot of prayer."

"She's on my list." His attention switched to Callie. He reached inside his light jacket and pulled out a large envelope. "I have some pictures I want you and Trace to look at. They just arrived from Saint Louis today." He handed it to her.

With Trace looking over her shoulder, so close his breath tickled her ear, and Jolene standing silently by, Callie pulled half a dozen photographs from the envelope. She flipped through them one by one, and then stopped to stare at the face she could not erase from her memory. Those cold eyes bored right through her from the paper. Her lungs constricted until she could hardly breathe. She looked up at Leon, gnawing her lip in indecision. Then she placed it on top of the stack and pointed. "That's him."

"He's the man I saw here at the school last Saturday," Trace added.

Leon's mouth formed a line that reminded Callie of a bent straw. "His name is Boomer Dutton. The Saint Louis police suspect he killed the man found dead in that hotel. He must have finally made a connection between the Cal who worked at the hotel and Callie who worked at the boardinghouse."

"But how would he have done that?" Trace asked.

Leon grimaced. "The police talked to the landlady, and she said a woman tried to rent a room from her a while back. Said she seemed real disappointed that there were none empty, but she was real chatty and said her friend Cal had recommended the boardinghouse."

Flashes of memory came to Callie. "Did Mrs. Thompson describe the woman? Did she wear a lot of beads and have bobbed hair dyed black?"

Leon nodded. "That's her."

Callie drew a deep breath. "It was Valerie Crandall. She works in the hotel office. I heard some of the other workers talking one day, and someone said her boyfriend was a gangster. It must have been Mr. Dutton they were talking about."

"When the woman said she wondered where her friend Cal had gone," Leon continued, "the landlady thought it was an affectionate nickname for you and said she supposed you must have gone back to Deer Lick."

"And finding your home would have been easy once Dutton knew your hometown," Trace added.

Leon nodded again. "Although he may be in the area to silence you, I can't help wondering if he's tapping local sources of booze while he's here."

Callie frowned and raked a finger over her lower lip. "You think there are already Saint Louis buyers doing business here?"

"I'm afraid so. And competition is fierce. If another outfit learned of the stills in these hills, they wouldn't hesitate to move in and set out to beat the competition."

This sounded scarier than ever. Callie shivered. "Do you have any idea who's involved?"

Leon scraped a hand across his jaw. "I wish I did. With Prohibition, producing alcohol's illegal. We find stills and destroy them, but new ones pop up. Someone's helping the locals stay in business. I'd sure like to figure out who. But that's my problem. Yours is to stay as invisible as possible and hope this guy buys the story that your brothers are no longer around."

Callie handed the pictures back to him. "I'll be careful. I am being careful. That's why I wore this ugly bonnet today."

He tucked the envelope back in his pocket, said, "Thanks," and left.

The day was a bigger success than they could have hoped for. After people cleared out, Callie eyed the surplus of items still on the tables. "What are we going to do with this stuff?"

Jolene shook her head. "I don't know. There's so much of it that I don't have any place big enough to store it while we figure out good homes for it all."

"You know I don't. Our house is small, and the shed between the house and barn is full of sawmill gear and supplies. The barn has no extra space, either."

"There's a room at the back of the dealership that I could empty."

Both girls spun to face Trace.

"You'd do that?" Callie asked in surprise.

He grinned. "Only if you two help load it into my truck. And you—" he indicated Callie "—ride to town with me to help me put it away."

"Of course we will. Won't you, Callie?" Mischief gleamed from Jolene's eyes.

Callie recognized manipulation, but she couldn't turn down such an offer. "Okay. But I'll have to take the buckboard home first."

Jolene went to the door and stuck her head out. "Irene, come help us get ready to go."

It didn't take them long to carry everything out and put it in the back of Trace's truck. Irene carried her share. Then she went back outside while the adults put the room back in order.

"We'll see you tomorrow at church," Jolene called through the open window of her car as she and Irene drove away.

Callie felt awkward now that she and Trace were alone. She hesitated on the school steps.

When he smiled at her, she wanted to turn away, to escape those penetrating blue eyes. But she had no choice but to face him and deal with the nervousness she felt just being in his presence.

"I'll help you hitch the horses," he said and went to do it. After the buckboard was ready, he gave her a boost up onto the seat.

"I'll be right back," Callie said as she clicked the horses into motion. She drove across the road and pulled up in front of the house just as her dad emerged from it.

"If you're done with them, I could use 'em." He nodded at the buckboard and team.

Grateful to not have to unhitch them, Callie hopped to the ground. "I need to go back to the school." She handed him the reins and headed back across the road.

"Come on." Trace placed a hand across her back as he met her at the edge of the schoolyard.

Callie nearly jumped out of her skin and set off at a pace just fast enough to get beyond his unsettling touch.

He caught up with her and opened the truck door. She crawled inside and sat stiffly, staring straight ahead, while he went around and got behind the wheel. When his head turned, she quickly looked away, unable to maintain eye contact. Being in a confined space with him made that space feel even smaller.

The three-mile drive was a mixed experience for Callie. Her nervousness kept her from enjoying the rare opportunity to ride rather than walk. She drew a breath of relief and hopped out of the truck when Trace parked behind the auto business.

He removed the tarp that covered the goods in the back

and handed Callie a load. Then he got his own load and led her to the back door of the building.

"We'll put it back here." He reached around her to ease the door open.

The large room they entered was clearly a junk room. Boxes and loose items were piled along one wall. A long table stretched along another. Scraps of lumber and a film of fresh sawdust littered it.

"Looks like you've been working." She indicated the sawdust.

"I've got my display case framed. Hopefully I can finish it this week. Let's pile as much as we can on here." Trace put his load down and emptied Callie's arms.

It took them several minutes to get everything inside. When they finished, they both stood back and gazed around. Trace grimaced. "I'll try to get this place a little more organized, but right now I'm hungry. How about you?"

Callie shrugged. "Not too much. I'll eat when I get home."

"Will you let me take you to the restaurant and buy you lunch?"

She backed up a step, shaking her head. He couldn't possibly want to be seen in public with her.

"I promise I'll only bite the food. And I can't take you home hungry."

She rolled her eyes upward, recognizing persistence. "You don't need to feed me. You've already given your money and your work. And this." She moved a hand in an arc that encompassed the room.

"Pretty please."

She snorted. "You're too used to getting your way."

But the thought of food and something to drink made her mouth water.

He gave her a quirky grin. "Am I going to get it this time?"

She hesitated only another moment. "All right."

He ushered her back out the way they had entered. They circled the building to the sidewalk and strolled past the shuttered showroom window. Like several other businesses, the car dealership closed at noon on Saturdays.

"Dad works Saturdays," he said, reading her mind. "I work full-time all week, but he only works mornings, unless something comes up and he decides to change his hours."

She nodded and kept pace. "He's giving you more responsibility."

At the restaurant they took a table near a window with a view of Main Street. "Order whatever you want," he said quietly.

Callie gulped and studied the prices posted on the wall. They represented enough money to buy groceries for a week. "I'll just have a sandwich."

He reached over and placed a hand over hers. "Let me feed you. I'll order." He stared into her eyes for a moment that went on too long. Callie's face blazed with heat.

Her heart stuttered, and she pulled her hand away. She shook her head in defeat and fought to keep her voice steady. "Give an inch, you take a mile."

"Good."

He ordered the special—pork roast, mashed potatoes and gravy, and peas. Callie bowed her head to whisper a silent blessing, but Trace surprised her by speaking one aloud.

After they finished the meal—which made her feel

more full than she had in months—and Trace paid the bill, they headed back down the street. Callie felt relief that they had not encountered any family or close friends. She felt conspicuous, but warm from his attention. Back inside the truck, she sat near the door and watched the landscape slip past. Sumac, sassafras and Virginia creeper had started to paint it with color.

He turned onto the gravel road. "Do you know how to drive?"

She twisted around to face him. "Not a car or truck. I've driven the tractor."

"Then it's time you did."

He pulled the truck to the side of the road, stopped and turned off the motor. Then he got out and came around to Callie's side of the vehicle. When he opened the door, she just sat and stared at him.

He held out a hand. "Come on."

She shrank back. "I can't drive your truck. I might wreck it."

"No, you won't." He waggled his fingers.

She hesitated only a moment longer, unable to pass up such an opportunity. Then she hopped out and went around and got behind the wheel.

"Okay, let's go."

He showed her how to turn on the gas, push the timing lever and pull out the throttle. "You don't need to use the choke since the motor's already warm."

Callie nodded and pushed the clutch pedal all the way to the floor.

"You're ready to start it now."

She pressed the starter and clenched her hands on the steering wheel when the engine came to life.

"Ease out on the throttle."

She did as he instructed and let up on the clutch. The truck lurched and died.

He laughed, a pleasant sound. "Try again, and don't let the clutch out so fast."

She did, and the truck rolled down the road this time. A thrill of exhilaration whizzed through her, making her grin like an idiot. "This is fun." She peered intently at the road ahead.

Trace watched the glow on Callie's face, and his breath caught. An unexpected adolescent longing struck him. No, it was an adult attraction, plain and simple. The realization made him look at her with fresh eyes.

She couldn't be described as a breathtaking beauty, but she was pretty as pie, as his dad would say. An urge to make her smile more often came to him.

Then confusion clouded his brain. He couldn't afford to feel such things. His past was already murky with a lost love and a failed relationship. He would never find perfect love again, not a love he could lose.

When Callie braked to a stop in front of her home, he detected a reluctance to have the ride end. He shared it. They faced each other, and both started to speak. But the sound of a slamming door interrupted them. They looked around to see an angry little sister stalking toward them from the mill where Mr. Blake was loading lumber onto the wagon Callie had used and returned that morning. Clem wore a glower that made Callie sigh aloud. She started to get out. "I may as well see what bee's under her bonnet."

"So you sicced the marshal on us. Some sister you are," Clem shouted, blocking the door.

"No, I didn't," Callie denied her accusation.

This little sister must be as rowdy as he had heard. "Why do you think she did that?" he asked, inserting himself into the conversation.

Clem glared at him, arms raised and hands clenched. "He came over here to talk to me and Delmer."

He looked at her wrists. "You don't seem to be under arrest."

He thought he detected a tiny twitch in the corner of Callie's mouth.

Clem looked from him to Callie, and then back. "What are you doing here?"

"Giving your sister a ride home."

"Hmph. That thing at the school ended two hours ago. Where you been?"

"It's none of your business," Callie snapped. "But we had to store the leftover stuff. What did the marshal talk to you about?"

Clem tossed her head and tilted her nose. "He said Delmer should stay out of sight. He said I should stay home more, too, but it's none of his business where I go or what I do."

"It is if you hang around where you shouldn't be and do things you shouldn't do. And I didn't have to tell him anything about you. He knows everything that goes on around here."

That statement seemed to give the girl a jolt. She turned and flounced away.

Callie sighed again and gave him an apologetic look. "I should—"

"Would you like to go for a walk?"

Chapter 7

She would love it, but the idea was foolish. The knowledge didn't stop her, though. She eyed his casual clothing and couldn't prevent a grin. "You up to hiking in the woods?" She hopped to the ground.

"You bet." He got out and met her in front of the truck.

Callie forced herself to be calm, not let his nearness make a complete ninny of her. "You're welcome to come inside while I change clothes. It'll only take a couple of minutes."

"I'll wait for you here. No point disturbing your family."

She ran into the house, did an extra speedy change into the overalls she wore for farm chores or frogging and ran back outside without speaking to anyone. Trace knelt by her mother's late-blooming black-eyed Susans, pulling weeds from around the stems. He turned at her approach, and grinned. "Those overalls sure look better on you than your brothers."

Callie ignored the comment and headed across the yard. "Come on."

He caught up with her as she struck out for the east pasture. She led him through a wooden gate that was wide enough for the tractor to drive through and tramped through the field of cornstalks.

"Where are we going?"

"For a walk. Isn't that what you wanted?"

He chuckled. "I didn't expect you to walk my legs off."

At the far side of the timber-bordered field they crossed the fence and entered the woods onto a barely visible footpath. She pointed at the lane they passed. "The Lonigans live up there."

He surveyed their surroundings. "Do you think they have a still back here?"

"They did, but I suspect they've moved it again." She didn't explain that Clem and Delmer had probably helped them do it.

"So we're looking for the new location of their still."

She nodded while peering ahead, debating which way to go.

"Do you know where you're going?"

She turned to face him. "Nope. But I figure if we loop around behind their place we're bound to find something." She took off again.

"Ah, gotcha," he said to her back.

They plowed on through the woods, pushing back branches when necessary. When they emerged into a clearing, she studied the ground. "Here's where it was."

He peered where she pointed. "I see what you mean. The ground is disturbed, and they left behind some debris."

He picked up a piece of tubing and a strip of wood that looked like a piece from a barrel stave.

Callie studied the lay of the land. Then she set out again, still heading east.

They passed an unused road that had grass growing down the center of it. Then they hiked for about a quarter of a mile parallel to Deer Creek until a thick stand of brush caught her attention. They fought branches and worked their way inside the area to an open space. It held a still.

A flat tin roof had been laid over a crude pole frame. Barrels of various sizes sat in a haphazard cluster. A cooker held place of honor at the right front of the shelter. To one side Callie spotted a rough board bench. She couldn't imagine drinking anything, let alone alcohol, that had been made in these unsanitary conditions.

Trace whistled. "Leon needs to know about this."

Callie faced him, a hand under her nose to block the smell. "I'll leave that to you."

He studied her expression. "Would you prefer that I not mention your part in finding it?"

She shrugged and grimaced, realizing that he understood. "They're my neighbors."

"I'll stop by his place on my way home."

They left the thicket, and Callie pointed ahead. "Let's loop around that way. It's smoother ground for walking, and we'll make better time."

"Are you in a hurry?" he asked without breaking pace.

She slowed a little. "I guess not. But there's always work I could be doing to help Mom."

"You work very hard, don't you?"

She shrugged. "My dad says 'them that don't work

don't eat.'" She huffed out her chest and imitated his gruff manner and deep voice the best she could.

Trace's hearty chuckle made her heart sing. "The Bible does say something like that. But I bet your parents would like for you to relax once in a while."

She stole a peek at him, the butterflies in her stomach addling her. She had had a little-girl crush on him from the age of seven. But she had gotten older, recognized it for the hero worship it had been and gotten over it. Now those feelings had resurrected full-blown.

Stop. He has his life. I have mine.

Hollowness filled her middle at the picture of her future—alone. She concentrated on their surroundings, the cloudless sky, and the woods from which they had just emerged.

"I guess you'll be picking this soon." Trace indicated the rows of cornstalks.

"Probably next week, according to Dad."

"The work your family does is a lot more physical than selling cars."

Callie turned a mischievous look on him. "You look healthy enough."

He flexed his biceps. "Selling cars doesn't make me strong, but working on them does."

She feigned astonishment. "You mean you can make the things run? I don't believe it."

His eyes locked on her, and suddenly the mirth in them changed, became electric. His healthy good looks made her mouth go dry and her breath catch. She resumed motion with a bound, lunging forward and plowing her way through the stalks at a near-run.

When they broke into the open, Callie caught her breath. Beside her, Trace showed no signs of fatigue.

They had come out farther down the road than their starting point. They started to cross the fence to walk up the road the final hundred yards to the house.

Trace pushed the bottom strand of barbed wire down with his foot and pulled the middle one up with his hands. Callie stooped and lifted a foot to step through the opening. But a sound made her stop.

They both looked up to see a black car coming up the road.

Fear struck Callie like a bolt of lightning.

Please, no, Lord.

Trace released the strand of wire and glanced around. "Here you are, dressed like a boy, out in the open, and no bonnet."

The tense edge in his voice stabbed Callie with guilt. She didn't protest when he grabbed her hand and practically dragged her back into the corn patch. They worked their way into the stalks enough to crouch and peer out without being seen.

"Be still so the leaves don't move and draw attention," he whispered next to her ear.

Heart thumping, Callie peered out at the road. As the car puttered nearer, she held her breath. Then let it out in a long whoosh of relief when she recognized Pastor Denlow behind the wheel. "He must have traded cars. That's newer than the one he usually drives. Or maybe it's his brother's."

They both got up. Callie brushed at her dusty pant legs.

Trace looked behind them. "Why don't we go around through those woods and come up behind your house?"

"I'll beat you there." Callie set out at a run. She didn't have to look around to know Trace was right behind her.

Making no effort to be quiet, they circled around the field and came out just below the barn.

For a few stolen moments Callie let herself feel care-free and pushed away thoughts of threatening men and dangerous stills. God had given them this beautiful after-noon to enjoy. It would be a shame to waste it. She dashed across the barn lot and through the gate. Then she locked it and darted away before Trace caught up with her.

"You can't escape me, Callie."

Hearing him clamber over the wooden gate and drop to the ground, she veered to the left and ran past the smaller of the two sawdust piles. She stopped and lis-tened for footsteps, but didn't hear any. Suddenly Trace came running around the other side of the pile.

"Gotcha." He grabbed her arms and tumbled them back onto the soft heap of sawdust. Fragrant when fresh, it was far less pungent now.

Callie squealed and pushed at his chest. "Let me up, you big goon." She shifted sideways and twisted away from him. Then she scooted backward like an ungrace-ful crab.

Instead of pursuing her, Trace threw his hands over his head and flopped backward onto the sawdust. Callie drew her knees up and wrapped her arms around them, drinking in the sight of him as he worked his arms up and down like a bird flapping its wings. She grinned. "You look like a big kid making snow angels, only with-out any snow."

He went still and stared up into the sky. "I feel like one."

His voice held a quality that Callie couldn't quite in-terpret, an odd vulnerability. "You probably don't take time to play very often. Or you've forgotten how." She leaned her chin on her knees.

He turned his head, and his pupils darkened as their gazes met. The world seemed to shrink until there were only the two of them in it. His eyes traveled over her features one at a time. "You're good for me, Callie. You offer me friendship without consideration for what I can give you. That's rare."

Heart thudding, Callie didn't know quite how to respond. "Maybe we both need that kind of friendship," she breathed uncertainly.

He sat up and scooted closer, way too close, his gaze riveted on her. He reached for her hand, his gaze intensifying. Awareness pulsed between them as he gave the hand a light squeeze. Callie read in his expression that he felt it, too.

With his free hand he nudged her chin up, bringing their faces within inches of each other, so close she could feel his warm breath on her cheek. Her insides quivered like jelly.

He trailed a finger along the line of her lips, his breath making her cheek tingle. Callie couldn't think, couldn't get her breath. She wet her lips with the tip of her tongue, woozy from the rush of anticipation and pleasure that flowed through her with the force of an avalanche.

Suddenly he went still, as if struck by a dash of cold reality. Breathing quickly, he released her hand and literally threw himself back onto the soft bed of sawdust. Eye contact broken, he stared up at the clouds drifting across the sky.

"I don't have a good history with women," he said, as if speaking to himself.

Cheeks flushed, Callie eased back and put a few more

inches between them. "Your first fiancée didn't see you as someone to give her things, did she? I'm sorry," she said quickly. "I didn't mean to pry."

"If we're friends, you don't have to apologize for asking questions that rise from something I said." He spoke without looking over at her. But it wasn't a rude ignoring. It was more like he was taking a long look back at his past. "Joanna was sweet and wholesome. And she loved me."

"And you loved her."

He expelled a heavy sigh and spoke to the clouds. "We knew by our second date that we were meant for each other. We also knew we were too young to get that serious."

"I knew that," Callie said quietly. "I used to see you together sometimes when my parents took us all to town on Saturdays. Joanna was a very pretty girl."

She remembered watching them from a distance and envying Joanna Michaels. Joanna had been bright and popular, perfect for Trace, something she, Callie, would never be.

"I gave her a ring a year after we graduated from high school." His words slowed. "She wore it for a year and a half. One day two months before our wedding date I had just come home from a three-day meeting in Saint Louis, and her brother came to the house. When he asked me to come outside, I knew by his manner that something was wrong, but I couldn't have imagined how wrong. The first thing he did was hand me a ring box and explain that Joanna had asked him to return it to me. I was too stunned to even ask why."

Callie listened in silence, sensing that he needed to

talk about this, that it had been buried inside him for a long time.

After several moments, he continued, "I couldn't understand. After I absorbed the shock a little bit I made Jesse tell me why he was delivering it. He said Joanna was sick. She had scarlet fever, and their house had been quarantined. He wasn't home when it happened, so he was staying with a friend. His mother had called, crying, and said she was leaving the ring on the porch for him to pick up and bring to me. Joanna had made her do it. Said she wanted me to have it. I still do," he finished.

"It's been, what, five years?" Callie could hardly speak, her heart aching for him. She had still been in high school, but she remembered the mourning of the town.

"Yeah." He swallowed. "She died a few days later. I never saw her again."

Callie cleared her throat past the surge of emotion. "I don't understand why God allows suffering, but I know He loves us and doesn't torture us for any unloving reason. I also know we can find comfort in the word of God, that sorrow can bring us closer to Him. Jesus said, 'Come unto me, all ye that labor and are heavy laden, and I will give you rest.'"

He raked a hand over his eyes. "I was bitter and did some things I'm not proud of. I ignored God and quit going to church. I couldn't pray. I didn't care what happened to me."

He turned his head and looked right at Callie. "I eventually became so desperate that I talked to the pastor. He helped me see that I will never understand, that I have no choice but to accept and go on with my life, and that God never left me when I left Him. But I refused to associate with women, thinking that part of my life was over."

"Until your parents pressured you."

"You know how my second engagement ended." His tone went flat, and he stared up into space again.

He seemed to retreat to somewhere she couldn't follow. But after a long pause he turned his head toward her again. The hollow look in his eyes gradually faded. Then a ghost of a smile lifted the corners of his mouth. "I have an idea, if you're willing to make a deal."

Callie straightened her knees and leaned back on her hands, not sure what to expect. "Let me hear it."

"I'll clean up and organize that room at the business, build some shelves and racks, so you can operate your swap shop out of there. I'll even talk to the town board and encourage members to donate goods for you to distribute to those who need them."

Callie tilted her head. "And what do I have to do for you in exchange?"

All hint of a smile disappeared. "Some of those goods need to get to Joanna's parents. The Michaelses have suffered from losing Joanna, and they haven't been doing well since the economy got so bad. Jesse has a family of his own that he's struggling to support."

The tightening in her chest made it hard for Callie to respond. "Of course I'll do that. But are you sure about letting us use your space?"

"I'm sure." The declaration rang with certainty.

"What will your dad say?"

Trace sat up. "He encourages civic involvement, and he's gradually turning the business over to me. So it's my decision regarding the building. The other item we discussed is a private matter."

Callie reached down and tugged off a shoe. "I think

Joanna would be pleased to know that you keep an eye on her parents."

Silence reigned for a long moment. "Do you think she knows?"

Callie nodded and shook sawdust from the shoe. "I think so. Moses and Elijah came down from heaven and met with Jesus and some of His disciples. Some people believe that, since they knew one another, people in heaven know what's going on down here on earth. I agree."

He stared upward into the heavens, a muscle in his jaw moving. "I find that comforting. Thank you for the thought."

Callie started to put the shoe back on, but then changed her mind. Instead, she pulled off the other one and wiggled her toes in the sawdust.

Trace stood and dusted off his pants.

An awkward moment fell between them. Callie got to her feet. "My brothers and sisters and I used to play on these all the time." She indicated both piles.

He looked up at the top of the one they were on. "I can picture you climbing this and sliding or rolling down it."

She grinned a challenge at him. "Care to try it?"

He looked down at her bare feet, debated a moment and then plopped back down to take off his own shoes.

"That's right. You have to feel it between your toes to really enjoy it." She turned and started to climb.

Trace spent the evening working in the storage room. While he labored, his mind worked just as hard. It had been fun romping on the sawdust pile with Callie, the freest he had felt in a long time. She was refreshing. He remembered the little girl Callie had been, so small, pretty and vulnerable with those haunting black eyes. The girl may have grown up, but those black eyes still haunted him.

Callie didn't have his last fiancée's delicate beauty, but her appeal far surpassed Beulah's. She stirred him, brought to life feelings he had thought long dead. It resembled what he had known with Joanna, but it had a newness to it that thrilled—yet scared—him.

He hammered at the nails with fervor, as if the action would chase the images and feelings from his mind and body. But they persisted. Callie had grown up and matured into a soft, natural kind of beauty. No longer skinny, she had a finely sculpted face, hair so black it held bluish glints and those deep, watchful eyes that had the power to mesmerize him.

He gave the hammer a mighty swing.

"Yee-ow!"

The tool flew from his hand, and he grabbed his thumb. He stuck it in his mouth, and then took it out and rubbed it fiercely. "Oh, that hurts," he groaned to the empty room.

Lord, I wanted distraction. But I didn't want it to hurt.

Callie brushed the skirt of her blue gingham dress into place, her thoughts drifting as she sat with her parents in church. Clem and Delmer sat in the very back with the younger set.

A movement behind them made her peek over her shoulder. Her eyes widened as Trace Gentry slipped into a rear pew the other side of the aisle. He nodded a slight acknowledgment as his blue eyes zeroed in on her. She flushed and faced forward.

What was he doing here at the mission church? He

couldn't possibly be pursuing her. The idea was ridiculous. He could date any single woman around. Still, she detected a speculative gleam in her mother's eye.

Callie kept her face aimed straight ahead throughout the service. At the end of it, Pastor Denlow announced there would be a workday to repair storm damage to the church.

As Callie exited, Trace appeared at her side. Her heart pounding, she forced herself to speak. "It's nice to see you today. Did you take a wrong turn?"

He shook his head. "No, I just felt I needed a change."

Jolene joined them and curved an arm around Callie's waist. "I hoped I would catch up with you. How is Riley doing?"

"He's much better, but the marshal wants him to stay out of sight."

"I'm glad to hear he's better."

"Trace has offered us a room to hold our swap meets and store leftovers."

Jolene's face brightened. "Oh, good." She grabbed his hand and shook it. "Thank you."

Callie's mother appeared beside her. "Will you and Mr. Gentry come eat dinner with us?"

"Thank you, Mrs. Blake, but I can't impose on you." Trace spoke to Dessie, but his eyes locked on Callie.

"You're more than welcome, and we have plenty," she insisted.

Jolene looked from Trace to Callie. "I fixed dinner for my family this morning before I left, so they're taken care of. If Mr. Gentry can come, I can take Irene home to eat with the folks and come right back."

"I made a blackberry cobbler last night." Callie's voice came out scratchy.

Trace focused on her. "I'll come if you'll ride with me to your house."

"Glad to have you, young man." Arlie approached just in time to prevent her refusal.

Trace enjoyed the meal more than any in a long time. Riley, wearing unbuttoned pants with a shirt hanging loosely over them, came to the table. Trace couldn't help but notice an odd sort of tension between Riley and Jolene as they sat side by side.

The cooking outdid his mother's, especially Callie's cobbler. The eight people around the table kept up a friendly chatter, although the two youngest ate quickly and left the house.

"Is there anything I can do?" Trace offered when they were gone.

"You can get those two out of the way." Dessie pointed at Arlie and Riley. "Take the chairs out in the backyard where it's not hot from cooking. We'll join you when we get this kitchen cleaned up."

Trace copied the two Blake men and picked up a chair in each hand. He followed them out the back door. They positioned the chairs under a big oak tree and settled to visit.

"Ah, this feels good." Arlie nearly moaned in pleasure as he sat down. "Don't get much chance for sittin'."

"So how's the car business?" Riley asked, his chair tipped back against the tree.

"Not bad. Money's tight everywhere, but people still find a way to buy cars."

The conversation moved on to the different models of cars and which each liked best. "I have to prefer Chevies since I make my living selling them," Trace commented, his eyes following Callie as the women came out to join them. "They're good to me, so I'm good to them. If you ever decide you're ready to buy one, let me know and I'll help you find a good deal."

Arlie's face creased. "I been thinking about trying to get one. I don't hardly see how I can do it just yet. How about a used one? Can you find one that's in good shape for a cheap price?"

Trace nodded, glad to find a possible way to help this hardworking man. "I'll keep my eyes open and let you know when I run across something I'd feel good about recommending."

"You talking about buying a car?" Dessie asked as she dragged a chair over next to her husband. She swatted away a bevy of flying insects before sitting.

Arlie's head bobbed. "I been thinking about it for a spell."

Suddenly the sound of gunshots echoed across the trees. Then a tremendous *boom!* shattered the air. Everyone jumped to their feet and gazed eastward to see smoke boiling from the trees.

Chapter 8

Callie's breath caught. Heart thumping, her eyes locked with Trace's in comprehension.

"It's the still," she whispered. "What should we do?"

Trace took control. "Jolene, go to the nearest phone and call Leon. Tell him the Lonigan still has exploded."

Jolene's eyes rounded in question, but she spun and ran to her car, Riley at her heels.

Mom grabbed Riley's arm, stopping him. "Don't go, son. You're already hurt."

"I'm going with Jolene." His tone was firm. He patted her hand and took off.

"I'll get a shovel," Arlie yelled. "You two run to the barn and get a load of them gunny sacks piled next to the feed bin."

Callie and Trace took off at a run. They each gathered an armload of sacks and headed back to Trace's truck.

By that time Dad and Mom had climbed into the back. Callie got in beside Trace.

"Do you think Clem and Delmer are over there?" he asked as he started the engine.

Callie saw no point in avoiding the question. "I'm afraid so." She prayed they weren't facing another tragedy. Fear knotted her stomach.

Trace drove to the rough road that led into the woods. Callie reasoned that other neighbors had heard the explosion and would respond, if they hadn't gotten there first. Trace's steady presence gave her a bit of calm.

Chances were strong that someone had gotten hurt. If the Lonigans were not among the injured, they would have fled. The smell of smoke reached them as the truck bounced to the edge of the thicket they had found the day before. Flames lapped up the dry grass in a widening circle.

Trace turned off the engine. Dessie and Arlie met them beside the truck, Dad wielding his shovel. "I'll start digging a trench while you two and Dessie beat out the fire. But first let's see if there's anyone hurt."

Callie ran to the still—or where the still had been. Scraps of wood and metal littered the clearing. A man lay where the cooker had stood.

Trace got to him first and dropped to the ground beside him. He checked for a pulse and turned to face them. "We can't help him. Let's tackle the fire."

"Who is he?" Mom demanded, nearly screaming as she ran up behind them, her face white with panic.

Trace shook his head. "It's not your son. I've never seen him before."

As they beat at the flames, a wagon pulled up behind

Trace's truck. Mr. and Mrs. Trexlar from across the valley got out and joined them in the battle.

"We have to get this out before it reaches the field," Dad called as he dug near them. "Thank goodness the leaves haven't fallen yet."

Callie watched for Delmer or Clem as she swung her sack and worked her way along the fire line. She wiped soot from her face and rubbed her burning eyes, choking on smoke. The sound of a moan made her go rigid. Which way had it come from?

"What is it? You hear something?" Trace asked at her side.

She nodded. "I think I heard somebody moan."

He glanced back to where her parents and the neighbors were putting things back in the truck and wagon. "Which way?"

Callie pointed toward the nearby creek. "I'm not sure, but I think from over there."

They walked in silence, peering around every tree and bush. When they reached the creek bank, a strangled sob rose in Callie's throat. *Oh, God, please don't let him be dead.*

"It's Delmer," she nearly screamed over her shoulder as she ran toward the body lying on its side next to the water.

Trace ran past her and knelt by the boy. A touch on Delmer's shoulder made him groan.

"He's alive," Callie choked in relief as she landed on her knees. She slid a hand under his head and raised it a bit.

"He's been shot in the thigh. There's also a graze on his neck."

"Delmer, can you hear me?" Callie whispered through a dry throat.

"Clem," he croaked. "That…you…Clem?"

"No, it's Callie. Where is Clem?"

He never opened his eyes. "Gone…for help."

At that moment Clem came crashing through the trees. "They weren't…" She stopped as she spotted Trace and Callie. Her dress was tattered, and her eyes red and puffy.

"Oh, thank God you're here." Her mouth quivered, and tears ran down her face. "Please tell me he'll be all right."

Trace looked around. "We have to get him to a doctor. You girls get his legs. I'll take his head and shoulders."

Lifting him brought another groan. They started through the woods and met Arlie and Dessie halfway back to the truck. Dessie burst into tears.

"What happened?" Arlie demanded.

"We were out here talking to Troy and Chuckie Lonigan," Clem explained as she trotted to keep up. "Mr. Lonigan and another man were busy at the…still. Another guy showed up and started to talk to them, but when he saw Delmer, he pulled out a gun and shot him. The man with Mr. Lonigan thought he was the one being shot at, so he pulled out a gun and shot back. Bullets hit the still, and it exploded."

As they reached the truck, Leon Gentry pulled up behind it and got out. He looked at Delmer and shook his head. "Fill me in quick. Did the guy who shot Riley do this?"

Clem started to speak, failed and had to try again. "Delmer started to run and said, 'It's him again.' Then a bullet hit him and he fell."

Callie and Clem let the marshal take their place and help Trace ease the wounded boy into the back of the truck. Their parents climbed in beside him and placed his head in Mom's lap.

"You get to the doctor. I'm going to talk to that cowardly Lonigan bunch." Leon aimed a stern look at Clem. "I'll talk to you and Delmer later."

"There's a blood trail leading away from here," Trace called back to them as he rounded the truck. "You might want to look for the second shooter first."

Leon nodded. "I'll have a look around, but I don't figure on finding him. There's no car around, so he must have been able to drive away. Ask Doc if he's treated any more gunshot wounds today. Tell him we're looking for a guy who goes by the name of Boomer Dutton."

Because his gun goes boom when he kills people? The thought made Callie sick.

Trace scooted behind the wheel and got them out of there.

"This is the second son you've brought in here with gunshot injuries. What's going on?" Dr. Randolph demanded when they got Delmer into his office.

"The same man shot both of them. Delmer got away after seeing him shoot Riley, so as soon as he saw Delmer today, he started shooting," Clem explained in a strangled rush.

The doctor nodded. "You folks go back out front. We'll give him something for the pain and get that bullet out of his leg."

"I have to find Don Morley at the funeral home and send him out where this happened."

Trace's statement startled the doctor. "You mean there's another person out there?"

"Yes, but he's beyond your help."

"Another member of this family?" the doctor asked in disbelief.

Trace shook his head. "It's someone from out of town."

"Bootleggers?" The doctor pointed at something he wanted his nurse to hand him.

"I think so. Sorry to run, but I have to find Don." Trace turned to Callie. "I'll be back to take you all home."

Once again Callie found herself seated in the front room of the doctor's quarters, waiting in tense silence with her parents and sister. When the doctor finally came out, they all stood.

"He's weak, but the bullet's out, and he's patched up. The biggest concern now is to keep the wounds clean and free of infection. You may take him home as soon as your ride is ready."

Trace lay in bed that night, a picture of Mr. and Mrs. Blake invading his mind. They were poor people, but hardworking and uncomplaining. It troubled him that life had been, and continued to be, so hard for them. Never in his life had he experienced this kind of genuine compassion for the well-being of others. He had never wished bad for anyone. He just never got personally involved in the lives of others. He basically just tossed some money into the pot when someone asked for a contribution, but remained blind to the details of the needs of those with far less than he had always had and taken for granted.

Each person should do as he has decided in his heart—not out of regret or out of necessity, for God loves a cheerful giver.

The words came to him as if directly from God. "God, this feels different, maybe even cheerful. It feels good. I've always done charitable acts, but not necessarily for

the right reasons. Helping with Callie's swap has no motive connected to the business. I'm helping because I
want to."

*My child, what you are doing is good. But don't boast
of your good works.*

The words came to mind in a vaguely chiding way. "I
understand, Lord. Forgive me for being so blind. Show
me how to help others, from the heart."

Monday after work Trace attended the town board
meeting and convinced the community leaders to donate
ten dollars and their support to the swap meet opera-
tion. Leon caught him at the door as he left the meeting
and slapped him on the shoulder. "Good to see you getting more personally involved in the community, little
brother. And I approve of your new female interest. That
little gal is all right."

Trace snorted. "She's a friend." He didn't bother to
ask who Leon meant.

"A good friend to have. I wish you luck."

Under that kind of teasing Trace hesitated to bring up
the question he wanted to ask. But need overrode pride.
He stopped beside his truck. "Did you say you ordered
a new ice chest?"

Leon followed him to the side of the truck. "Sure did.
It arrived Friday. It's one of those Top-Icers with some
refrigerator features. Sharon loves it."

"Uh, what did you do with your smaller one?"

Leon's head tipped, and his eyes narrowed in shrewd
speculation. "You got a need for it?"

"I might. How much do you want for it?"

Leon looked up into the darkening sky and rolled
his tongue around inside his lower lip. "If you intend

to give it to the family I think you do, I don't want anything for it."

Trace ran a hand over his mouth. "I'll be happy to pay you for it."

Leon waved a hand in a dismissive gesture. "Aw, come get the thing."

"Thanks," Trace said simply.

Leon placed an arm on the roof of the truck and leaned against it, his expression sober. "I arrested Mr. Lonigan and his two boys last night. Then today I stopped by the Blake house. Delmer is already sitting up and talking. Carefully, of course. He wasn't hurt as bad as Riley."

"I'm happy to hear that."

"I'm sure you are. I plan to go back out there tomorrow and get down to business with him and the girl."

"Do what you have to do. I think the parents will be hurt, but they'll support you. They can't pay any fines, though."

Leon nodded. "I'll figure it out."

"Have you found out who the dead man is? Was?"

Leon grimaced. "His name is…was…Clyde Wilson. A couple of people admitted they've seen him around here before. He's a buyer for one of the Saint Louis outfits. Which means he must have a local connection. Dutton—the one who came here to shoot Callie—must have found out about the stuff in these hills and decided to move in on Wilson's territory. We still haven't found hide nor hair of him."

"He's wounded. He should have found a doctor."

"I talked to Doc Randolph, and he says he's had no gunshot victims besides Delmer."

Leon pushed away from the truck. "I need to get going."

* * *

"I'm sure your parents love you two very much, and I have no doubt they have taught you the difference between right and wrong and to respect the law." Marshal Gentry addressed Clem and Delmer, who sat in chairs facing him.

All defiance wiped from her face, Clem stared at the floor.

"Unfortunately, you chose to ignore the law and got involved in a dangerous situation. You're both under arrest."

Callie's heart ached as her mom gasped and covered her mouth with a hand. Dad pulled her to him. "It'll be okay," he said gruffly, his face haggard.

Callie thought of her little savings. She didn't have nearly enough to pay fines for both of them. Even if she did, she shouldn't. If they were old enough to break the law, they were old enough to answer for those actions.

Apparently her parents felt the same way. Neither offered any argument.

"Do you understand?" Leon asked when no one moved. He stared at Clem.

She looked up and nodded as if her neck were stiff, and then dropped her gaze to her hands. She looked distant and impassive, except for the single tear that trailed down her cheek.

"No!"

All eyes turned to Riley.

"It wuz Delmer and me let Troy and Chuckie talk us into helping them sell their stuff. After that guy shot me, Clem took my place. I didn't know she had done it, but it's all my fault."

Callie watched her baby sister face Riley, and it seemed she visibly grew up in those few seconds.

"You didn't make me do it," Clem declared through trembling lips. "It was my idea. Those bullets you took have punished you enough. Taking your place was my idea. I'm responsible for me. And I'm not going back to school, anyhow," she concluded.

Riley stared at her for what seemed forever, and then he looked over at Delmer. "Don't worry about the mill. I'll be going back to work tomorrow."

"You're not ready," Callie protested.

"I'm needed, so I'm ready," he declared resolutely.

Clem jumped up and ran to Riley. She fell to her knees and put her arms around him. "Thank you for trying to help me." When she got up, she faced the marshal. "Can't you let Delmer stay here? He's hurt."

Leon shook his head. "Afraid not. But you'll be together. You can take care of him." He went to Delmer and helped him to his feet.

Callie swallowed hard and bit down on her lower lip to steady it as she watched the marshal steer her younger siblings out the door, Delmer supported between Leon and Clem.

Just as they reached the gate, a truck came speeding down the road. Everyone halted in their tracks as it pulled in and stopped. Trace Gentry loped around the front of the vehicle and stopped. He yelled at Leon, but his eyes gravitated to Callie.

"I think they've found the missing gunman."

Chapter 9

Trace watched Callie's face erupt into wide-eyed fear, and then evolve into tight-lipped resolve. She would face whatever she must with courage. Good. But he wanted to spare her.

He aimed his words at Leon. "Nolan Trexlar came to town to find you. When he couldn't, he came to my office and asked if I could get a message to you. He found a car in the woods while he was out hunting. He said it looked like the driver missed a curve, grazed a tree and rolled down a hill into some brush that nearly hid it. There's a dead man behind the wheel."

Leon turned to Dessie and Arlie Blake. "I'll come back for these two when I'm done." He sprinted toward his car.

Callie shot out the door and came toward him. "I'm going with you."

Trace shuddered inwardly at the thought of what she

might see. "You don't need to. You identified the picture, and I saw the man at the school. We can identify him."

She hesitated, clearly torn. "Thank you." It came out in a whisper.

He got back in his truck and drove after Leon and Mr. Trexlar.

The next day, sorrow warred with relief as Callie woke to memories of yesterday's events. Trace and Leon had confirmed that the dead man was the killer she had seen. It felt incredibly good to no longer have to live in fear. But her younger brother and sister had been brought to jail, and Callie's parents were heartbroken.

She forced the memories to the back of her mind and crawled into her overalls. Duty called. After breakfast she went to work at the mill.

By the end of the day she could hardly put one foot in front of the other. When she started across the field to the house, she stumbled and almost collapsed. Riley's arm came across her shoulders to steady her. He looked as tired as she felt.

"You've been good help, sis," he said gruffly. "Go on to the house. I'll chore with Dad."

She studied his drawn face. "You need to get off your feet."

He managed a grin. "I will when we're done."

Remorse rolled over her again. "You should never have been hurt. It's my fault."

The grin disappeared. "Stop that kind of thinking. You weren't to blame for seeing a murder while doing your job. Besides," he added, the grin returning, "I was getting stir-crazy. We don't have to stay out of sight anymore. I'm glad you're safe—and back home," he added in a husky tone. With a quick squeeze to her shoulders, he headed for the barn.

Touched by his unaccustomed show of affection, Callie blinked tightly and struck out for the house. She and Mom had supper on the table by the time Dad and Riley came in. But without Delmer and Clem, the house had an emptiness to it. They each darted looks at the vacant places at the table, but no one mentioned the kids being in jail. Callie knew, though, that Mom had driven the wagon into town that morning and taken them a packet of food.

Thursday was a repeat of Wednesday—until they got home for supper. They were at the table when a car pulled up in front of the house. Dessie went to the window— and gasped. "It's the marshal, and he has the kids with him." She flew to the door.

Leon Gentry ushered Clem and Delmer into the house ahead of him, and waited patiently at the side of the door while they accepted a hug from their mother.

"These two have been released," he said slowly, glancing around at the group who had migrated from the kitchen. "But there are conditions.

"They will be donating their services to work projects in the community. I'm to keep a record of the time they spend and the kind of work they do. The judge will decide when their debt is paid. And…"

The marshal paused and gave the two offenders a stern glare. "If either of them is caught near a still, or in possession of products from a still, they will return to jail immediately and stay there for six months."

"We understand." Delmer spoke for them, and Clem nodded agreement.

"Then I'll be going."

Suddenly he was gone, and the family was a unit again.

"You two get in here." Mom dabbed at her eyes with her apron and bustled about setting two more plates at the table.

The two ate as if starved. "Missed your cooking, Mom," Delmer paused to say.

Saturday morning Callie and Clem drove the buckboard to town for the swap meet. A sad-faced Jolene had stopped by Thursday to report that her mother was not expected to live. Callie promised to fill in for her mournful friend at school and to visit her ailing mother as much as she could. Surprisingly, Clem had offered to work today in Jolene's absence.

Trace waited in his truck for them when they pulled in behind the dealership.

"Whoo-hoo," Clem exclaimed when he ushered them inside. "This is great." She scanned the table and shelf-filled room.

"Choose a table for canned goods and put those on it." Callie indicated the jars of pickles Clem carried.

Trace moved close to Callie and spoke in a low voice. "I have some things in my truck I want you to see. I put a big sign in the window of the dealership directing people back here."

Callie watched his lips move, drowning in the scent that was distinctly his. Unable to speak, she dragged her gaze from his and followed him back outside to his truck. He climbed up into the back of it and pulled a tarp off something. "This was donated by someone. Would you like to have it for your parents?"

Callie stared at an ice chest, an item she had heard her mother wish for more than once. She heaved a deep breath and backed away. "I can't take that. You've done too much for us already. Give it to someone who needs it."

"I am. Your parents don't appear to me to have one. This is from someone who doesn't need it. Don't let your prickly pride keep your parents from having something they need."

He made it sound so simple. He didn't realize how his generosity affected her. How it made her want…well, too much.

"I'll leave it in the truck," he said, taking her acceptance for granted. "I'm going out to help the men fix the storm damage to the church, but I'll be back by the time you girls are done."

Knowing she was bested, Callie swallowed and whispered a simple, "Thanks."

He started to go around the truck, but stopped and took something from his pocket. "The town board asked me to give you this for this project." He handed her some money.

Callie gasped. "What's it for? What am I to do with it?"

"See that it gets where it's needed most. A couple of suggestions were putting gas in cars for people and paying doctor bills."

"Not Delmer's doctor bill. I'll pay that."

He nodded. "I know. Just like you paid Riley's. Pay someone else's."

She drilled Trace with a glare. "Are you sure this didn't come from you?"

He raised his palms. "I'm sure. The board voted to help you with this project because they think it's a good idea, and they like the way you've stepped up to help others. I wouldn't be surprised if some of them show up with personal donations."

As if summoned, a car came around the corner and pulled in. A wagon followed it.

"It looks like you're getting busy. I'll see you around noon."

Callie unhitched the horses and tethered them near a big oak tree.

Hours later, Trace smiled as he drove back to town from the church. He could swear that Callie Blake got prettier every time he saw her. She had matured so well from the girl he remembered from high school. Something about her drew him, stirred him. It made him happy to do things that would help her and her family. Every time he was near her he wanted to comfort her, protect her, to kiss her.

You just got out of one bad relationship. Stay away from her. Loving another woman is too risky. Haven't you learned your lesson?

Common sense returned. Callie was safe now. He no longer needed to protect her.

But who will protect me from her?

When he walked into the "swap room" he spied Clem snipping the hair of a man seated in a chair with a towel draped around his neck. A sign announcing Free Haircuts graced the wall behind them.

He approached Callie. "How did it go?"

She paused in bagging leftovers and looked up, a sparkle in her eyes that made his heart rate run amok. She pulled a knotted handkerchief from the pocket of her simple lilac gingham dress. "The mayor put a jar labeled Donations on a table and dropped a quarter in it. More people added money to it. With what you gave me from the town board, we have twelve dollars."

He smiled, happy because she was happy. The sight of her gorgeous, shiny eyes had him melting like a chunk of ice dropped on a hot stove. He struggled to speak. "They know you'll put it to good use."

Worry lines creased her face. "I can't carry this around with me, and I don't feel right about taking it home. It needs to be kept where…where I…"

"Where your integrity can never be questioned," he finished for her. "I understand. There's a small safe in my office. Would you like to put it there?"

She nodded, clearly relieved. "Yes, please." She unknotted the hanky and handed him the money.

"Come with me." He escorted her through a door into the showroom where his dad had already locked the front doors and gone home. He went inside his office and knelt to unlock the safe hidden behind a lower shelf. When he placed the money inside it and turned around, Callie was no longer in the doorway. He locked the safe and got up.

He found her in the showroom examining one of the two vehicles displayed there. She peered inside it at the interior.

"Want to see it from the inside?"

She jerked upright, startled. Then she grinned. "Sorry. You caught me snooping. But yes, I'd love to see it from the inside."

"Just a moment." He went to the Peg-Board at the back of the room and selected the correct key. When he returned and opened the door of the aquamarine car, he watched her inhale the whiff of new leather and fabric.

She slid gingerly onto the seat and gripped the wheel, her head moving in a circular motion as she took in the details of the interior. A hand slid over the passenger seat in a caress so loving it made him wish that hand would stroke his face.

She leaned her head back and looked up at the roof. It was impossible to miss the longing in her gaze. She turned to face him. "I love the Chevrolet Superior Series. It's more mechanically sophisticated and offers a choice of colors."

Huh? She knew one car from another?

"It has some nice features," he said, fishing for more.

She nodded. "Yep. Seating capacity for five, balloon tires, four-cylinder engine, disc wheels, three-bearing crankshaft, cellular radiator…"

He began to laugh. Then he nodded at the truck next to it. "Want to look at that?"

She hopped out and followed him, eyes gleaming. When he got the key and opened it, she hopped in eagerly and gave it the same inspection. "These inline six-cylinder Stevebolt engines are wonderful, but it was the Superior that gave Chevrolet its first lead in sales over Ford. The Cast Iron Wonder last year topped the one million mark in its first year."

His grin broadened. "I'm impressed. Please don't decide to go into competition with me."

He stood there enjoying the view while Callie checked out the mechanisms. When she got out, he moved close enough to inhale her clean feminine scent. He could see the rise and fall of her chest, the pulse of her throat. He swallowed against his own dry throat, feeling like a young teenager again, and questioned what he wanted to ask.

"Someday I'll own one of these," she declared, pushing back a stray strand of hair.

"I believe you will." His words came out strained. The ensuing silence told him that she would be gone in a second. He blurted the thought in his mind.

"Callie…would you let me take you to the picture show, or wherever you might like to go, some night next week?"

He stared into her eyes, waiting. She stared back, not moving or speaking for several long moments. Then a look of regret flashed across her face. "I promised Jolene that I'll fill in for her at school starting Monday. Her mother is much worse. With her mother so sick, I need to help them in any way I can."

She paused for a breath. "I couldn't teach all day and then seek my own pleasure while they're in such trouble."

He took her hand lightly in his own. "I understand."

He did. She truly needed to devote time to her friend. But she also didn't trust his motives. He had rushed her to raise their friendship to a more personal relationship before she was ready.

"Hey, Callie. Where did you go?"

Clem's voice made them draw apart. A moment later Clem appeared in the doorway, and Callie left him to join her.

She had turned him down. But she didn't seem happy about it.

His shoulders slumped. Then he straightened them and drew a breath of resolve. There was more than one way to accomplish things.

Chapter 10

Callie's first day filling in for Jolene at school went well. At the end of it, she considered her next priorities. She and Clem had delivered surplus produce and household items Saturday afternoon, including a stop at the home of Trace's would-have-been in-laws. Mr. and Mrs. Michaels had been surprised, and it had taken some persuasion to convince them that the surplus garden produce would waste if they didn't help eat it.

Callie's mind automatically returned to Saturday and what had sounded like a request for a date from Trace Gentry. She must have misunderstood. She could only be grateful that she had not accepted, and then found out she had made a fool of herself. Well, he certainly wouldn't hang around any more after such a refusal.

She stepped through the doorway, and came to a stupefied halt. There Trace stood, backed up against his truck, gazing around as if he didn't have a care in the world. Callie concentrated on the door latch, but she could only spend so much time locking it. She drew a deep, fortifying breath and headed down the steps.

"Why, hello, Mr. Gentry. Have you gotten confused? It's not Saturday, so there's no swap meet here today."

He flashed a white-toothed grin and pushed away from the vehicle. "Didn't you call me?"

Callie frowned as he came toward her. "Of course not. I…" She stopped when she realized he was teasing her. "What in the world are you doing here?"

He stopped next to her and shrugged. "I thought it would save you time if I give you a ride to see Jolene." His face formed an expression of mock sorrow. "But I'm too tired to drive."

Callie rolled her eyes upward. "You're full of applesauce."

"But you *would* like to go for a drive and see Jolene, wouldn't you?" Another appealing grin. His eyes glinted as they swept over her.

Yes, she would. And it would get her there a lot faster than walking. Callie let her eyes meet his for a moment, and felt the by-now-familiar connection between them. She considered refusing, and gave up. The rascal knew she wanted to go see Jolene, and that she couldn't resist a chance to drive a motorized vehicle.

"Let's go." She set off and got in the truck. She placed the books she carried on the seat between them and gave the wheel a loving touch.

The drive went way too fast. When they got to the Delaney house, Irene spotted them from the clothesline along the side of the yard. The young girl came to greet them. "Jolene's in the house taking care of Mother. Dad's down at the barn."

"I'll go help your dad while Callie visits your sister." Trace struck out in that direction.

Callie followed Irene inside to a room where Jolene sat in a chair beside her mother's bed. She looked tired and sad. "What can I do to help?"

Jolene looked up. "Pray."

"I do that regularly. What else?"

Jolene's eyes went to the heap of soiled clothing and linens on the floor. "She can't keep anything down. I had to give her an extra dose of medicine so she could sleep."

Please, Lord, be with this family. Strengthen them.

Callie scooped up the laundry. "I'll take these outside and wash them."

"Not yet." Jolene patted the chair next to her. "Tell me how your day went at school."

"I'll get the wash water ready," Irene said from the doorway.

Callie smiled at her. "Thank you."

"She's been a big help through all this," Jolene said as her little sister disappeared. "She washes dishes and carries in wood without complaining."

Callie gave Jolene a quick summary of the day and then went to join Irene in the kitchen. An hour later Callie had clean linens hung on the line in the backyard. As she started back inside, she spotted Sam Delaney and Trace coming from the barn. She waited for them. "I'm ready to go home."

"She's my chauffeur," Trace told Sam with a chuckle.

The man smiled at Callie and shifted his full milk pail from one hand to the other. "Thanks for being such a good friend to my girl. She needs you right now."

"Tell her I'll be back every day if I can."

Callie enjoyed the drive home, but when she pulled up near her house, the life drained from her. "I'm afraid they're losing her this time," she said quietly without moving to get out.

Trace reached over and covered her hand on the steering wheel, his touch warm and comforting. And more. "You're right. Sam told me the doctor said it's only a matter of time."

Tears stung Callie's eyes. She dragged in a calming breath and fought the knots of tension in her stomach— and the emptiness that struck her when his hand withdrew. A sudden urge to kiss him made her scoop her books, grab the door handle and scramble out before she could make a complete idiot of herself. She felt his eyes between her shoulder blades as she hurried to the house.

Tuesday Trace appeared after school again. And Wednesday.

"Don't you have a business to run?" Callie chided as she met him at the truck.

He shrugged. "Sales aren't exactly hopping these days. One person can keep track of everything. Dad only works half days, anyhow, and he said he doesn't care which half he works. So he's shifted to afternoons for a while."

He got in on the passenger's side. Recognizing a good thing when she saw it, Callie got behind the wheel and drove to Jolene's.

Isabelle Delaney looked so lifeless and frail that Callie couldn't bring herself to ask questions. She just went about helping Irene fix supper.

The rest of the week followed that routine. Saturday's swap meet had another good turnout, and Clem was a great help.

Callie knew as soon as she opened the schoolhouse door Thursday afternoon and saw Trace standing on the steps that he bore bad news. "Is it Jolene's mother?" she asked softly as students filed out past them.

"Ellen Dace called about an hour ago and said Jolene asked her to put out the word that her mother passed away this afternoon." The town's chief telephone operator often issued messages to the public for local citizens.

As soon as she could get ready, they headed to the Delaney house. When they got there, Callie knocked on the door and got no answer. "They'll be here soon," she stated with certainty. "They've most likely gone to the funeral parlor."

"You're right." Trace led her back to the truck. When they got in, he slid over close to her. She didn't protest when he placed an arm across her shoulders. His eyes held warmth that wrapped around her heart. His subtle masculine scent made her head swim.

"You and Jolene are very close, aren't you?" His pupils darkened as they traveled the features of her face.

She nodded, her nerve endings vibrating. She drew a deep breath before she could speak. "She's the best friend I've ever had. We went to school together, and she always treated me as an equal, never as poor white trash. She made me laugh, and we shared our dreams, our mistakes and our silliness. After high school we wrote each other regularly, and when I came back home we reconnected as if we had never been apart."

"I suppose you visited in her home and knew her parents well."

"We didn't spend a lot of time in each other's homes. We were too busy to run around much after school, but when I was at her house her parents always treated me with kindness. Isabelle has been ill for a long time, and Jolene has been more of a mother to Irene than a sister."

"You have taken care of your family, as well." He traced a finger along her jaw, their faces hovering mere inches apart.

Callie's lips tingled under his scrutiny, and her heart thudded inside her chest.

As his face moved nearer, she forgot to breathe. She was crazy to want him to kiss her, as he clearly intended to do. Yet she didn't pull away.

The sound of a car pulling in startled them. In an instant return to sanity they jumped apart. Callie scrambled to open the door and hurried to meet Jolene as she, her dad and Irene emerged from their car. All their eyes were red rimmed.

Callie wrapped her arms around Jolene. "I'm so sorry. Is there anything I can do?"

Jolene shook her head. "Take care of the school for me the rest of the week."

"You know I will, for as long as you want." She knelt beside Irene and opened her arms. The ten-year-old stepped into them and gave her a fierce hug.

Callie got up and extended a hand to Sam Delaney. "You have my condolences, sir."

"Thank you." He spoke gruffly and blinked his eyes. "The funeral will be next Saturday morning."

"If you'll lie down and get some rest, I'll go home and come back later with some food. I'm sure you'll have company arriving soon and don't need me underfoot."

Callie looked down at Irene. "Will you see that she rests? And you do the same."

Irene nodded and clutched Jolene's hand. "Yes'm."

The week passed in a blur for Callie. The funeral

Saturday morning was well attended, and most of the people followed the hearse to the cemetery. During those final moments at the graveside, Callie stared over at the location of her brother's final resting place and felt an extra bonding with her best friend, a joining in the heartache of loss. They went back to the Delaney house and worked side by side feeding people afterward.

"I can return to school Monday," Jolene said as they watched the last of the neighbors get in their cars and wagons to leave.

Callie could see that she was in no condition to return to work yet. "Why don't you let me do one more week so you can rest and spend extra time with your dad and Irene."

Jolene massaged her forehead. "Okay."

"Good." Callie gave her a hug.

Sunday morning during church Callie sat with her parents and sister, her mind drifting.

"Those motorcars so many of you drive need gas to run."

The pastor's words brought her to attention, as any conversation about cars tended to do.

"Without gasoline, a car will grind to a halt. So will you. We should fill ourselves with the gas of God's words and time in prayer. But don't just pray on Sundays, or when you're out of gas in your spiritual life. Prayer is not a 'spare tire' you can pull out when in trouble. It's a steering wheel that directs us along the right path all through the week."

Callie grinned slightly. Now she knew what was wrong with her. She was out of gas.

It really wasn't funny, though. She was tired of being poor, of being afraid of going hungry, of always hav-

ing to be strong and see that bills were paid, of never-
ending work.

*Lord, I'm empty. Please fill me, give me the strength
to do whatever I must.*

*Come unto me, all ye that labor and are heavy laden,
and I will give you rest.*

The remembered words from Matthew 11:28 com-
forted her.

Monday after school when she dismissed the students,
Callie was surprised to find Trace outside as usual. Confusion struck her. Uncertainty. She was thrilled to see
him. It was insane to continue this crazy pattern of contact. What did he want of her? Why didn't he stay away,
let her get over him?

"I don't need to go see Jolene every day," she said as
she approached him, proud of how steady she managed
to speak while everything inside fluttered and trembled.

He pushed away from the truck. "I know, but I wanted
to let you know that Leon made another arrest today. One
of our local residents made the mistake of meeting with
a crony from Saint Louis. The guy was mad over not
getting the load of stuff he had been promised from the
Lonigan still. He showed up in town and started giving
Dempsey a hard time about it."

Callie gasped. "You mean the Dempsey who bought
the hardware store last year?"

He nodded. "He moved here to find liquor sources for
his gangster bosses. He bought the store to give him a le-
gitimate reason for moving here, and access to information and connections. Anyhow, when the crony, who was
sent by their bosses, threatened him, they got in a fight.
Dempsey pulled a gun and shot the guy. Leon arrested

him. He'll be taken back to Saint Louis and turned over to the authorities there as soon as Leon can arrange it."

He got into the truck, waved and drove off, leaving Callie to absorb the implications of this latest news. It was another sign to try to get on with her life.

Clem bounced in excitement on the wagon seat beside Callie as they pulled up behind the dealership Saturday morning. "Oh, good. Trace is here."

She hopped down from the wagon before it had hardly stopped moving and rushed to where Trace waited near the back door to let them inside. As attractive as ever, he wore charcoal pants and a white shirt under a dark jacket.

Callie took her time unhitching the horses and leading them to a spot under some trees where there were still a few tufts of drab grass for them to nibble. She tethered them and returned to the wagon, sneaking a peek to see Trace turn from the door through which Clem had just disappeared.

He came to meet her. "Do you have things I can carry inside for you?"

Callie shook her head. "Only this." She indicated the single sack she had taken from beneath the seat.

He stepped a bit closer to her, which made her back up against the side of the wagon.

"I can't stay this morning, but I'm going to leave my truck here so you can use it to make deliveries after the swap meet." He pressed a key into her hand.

"I have the wagon," she pointed out breathlessly.

"But the truck is faster. And I know you like to drive it." A teasing grin accompanied the second sentence. "You can just bring it back here and leave it when you get done."

"But what will you drive?"

"I'll be fine. I have business here in town, and I can drive Dad's car."

A tiny flutter in her midsection made Callie almost dizzy. She sidestepped to go inside.

He placed a restraining hand on her arm. "There's something I want to ask you."

Callie went still, finding his face closer to hers than expected, and waited.

He reached inside his jacket pocket and pulled out a small packet. "A little bribe first."

Callie's eyes rounded. The sight of a candy bar transported her back to the time when a frightened seven-year-old watched her mortally injured brother get carried away, an eleven-year-old Trace befriended her and fed her a candy bar and her childish heart fell into his hands.

"You remember," she whispered, her salivary glands coming to life, unable to believe the message of remembrance in the darkness of his penetrating eyes.

"You were so sweet," he breathed in a husky voice. "So scared, and so hungry. Take it," he urged when she didn't move.

Callie swallowed, lost any will to resist and took the treat.

"Dad and I bought the vacant lot behind the business for parking space. I need to record the deed at the courthouse one day this week. Will you go with me? We can take a drive through the countryside afterward and enjoy the autumn foliage before the leaves die and the colors fade."

Callie couldn't move, speak or hardly breathe. At this point she would probably have agreed to jump into a well. "When?"

"Whatever day would work best for you."

His beautiful smile nearly blinded her. Her brain barely functioned, but her sense of duty brought her mother's face to mind. "Mom really needs my help Monday and Tuesday. Late in the week would be best."

"Friday, then. After our drive we can go eat somewhere."

She nodded mutely, wondering if she had lost her sanity. He hadn't used the word, but this sounded like a date.

"Callie!"

Clem's shout from the doorway broke the tenuous connection between them. Callie gave her head a quick shake and backed away. "Coming." She turned and fled inside, hoping her little sister didn't notice the flush in her cheeks.

Trace produced a satisfied grin at how he had convinced Callie to go out with him. It amazed him how the prospect of spending that much time with her made his heart beat faster.

He was moving on with his life—literally. He had found an older widow who wanted to take in a boarder to help her with expenses. He knew Mrs. Jenkins from church and was familiar with her difficult circumstances. It seemed a comfortable arrangement.

He inhaled the earthy fall scents as he carried his belongings from his truck into the house, whistling softly as a picture of Callie filled his mind. He knew by the way she blushed when he looked at her that he made her uncomfortable. He loved the way her midlength black hair framed her oval face. He loved the balance of high cheekbones and skin the color of cool cream. Her physical appeal surpassed any of the many pretty girls he knew, to be sure, but it was something deeper that drew him. An inner beauty and strength of character that the others lacked.

As he hung his clothes in the closet, the desire for a home of his own rekindled. Before Joanna's death he had bought a piece of property just outside the city limits and planned to build a house on it as soon as they could afford it. After her death he had dropped those plans and focused his attention on the business. Now the buried vision replayed in his mind. Could he afford it now? He thought so. He would start looking into the possibilities next week.

Chapter 11

September had slipped into October with hardly a no-tice. Then the temperature had dropped from the seven-ties to the fifties, and a blaze of color began to paint the countryside.

Callie's thoughts took a direction of their own. She hadn't told anyone about her date—or whatever it was—with Trace this coming Friday. She hugged the secret to herself.

His image haunted her. Those penetrating deep blue eyes under dark, even brows seemed to see right through her. His mouth didn't smile a lot, but when it did it daz-zled her. He was strong and capable of handling himself in any situation. But she also detected loneliness in him. Could he truly be interested in such a simple girl as her?

Callie forced herself to stop daydreaming and pay attention during church. She even stayed alert enough to detect a brief, puzzling encounter. She happened to glance back as Jolene entered the church, and saw Riley get up from the back pew and speak to her at the doorway. Jolene shook her head and answered briefly, then made her way to the pew where her dad and little sister sat. She would ask Jolene about it after the service.

"You're imagining things." Jolene's soft words held an underlying edge when Callie wondered aloud about the relationship between her best friend and her brother an hour later.

Callie studied the closed, sad look on her friend's face and didn't pursue the subject. The loss of her mother had to be affecting her deeply.

As the week passed, Callie grew quieter and more intense. Since asking her to go with him to the courthouse in Houston, she had heard nothing more from Trace. Her doubts renewed. What if he hadn't really meant it? What if she got ready and he forgot to show up?

That evening when the family had settled around the supper table, Dad said the blessing. Then he reached into his shirt pocket and took out a small envelope that had been folded into a square. He handed it across the table to Callie.

"I had to go to town this morning, and I met a friend of yours in the hardware store. He gave me this to give to you. I was in a hurry to get back and fix the steam engine, and I forgot."

Callie glanced at her name written on it and fought to steady her fingers and not drop it. She slid it under the edge of her plate.

"Well, open it, Cal. Tell us what your friend—" Delmer stressed the word "—has to say." His teasing voice was accompanied by a monkey grin.

Callie rolled her eyes and retrieved the envelope. She knew she would get no peace until she did. She opened it and pulled out a small piece of paper.

I'll pick you up at 12:30 Friday.
Trace

She returned the note to the envelope and shoved it back under the side of her plate.

"Well, what's he want?" Delmer demanded.

Callie shrugged. "My business."

Before she knew what was happening, he reached over and snatched the envelope. He waved it overhead. "Tell me what it says, or I'll open it. Did he ask for a date?"

She closed her eyes for a moment, and then reopened them. "No, he didn't. He just let me know what time he's picking me up Friday." She turned to Mom. "I won't be here for supper."

"You all be quiet." Dessie aimed her mama bear glare at Delmer and Clem.

That night Callie lay awake and stewed about what to wear Friday, not that she had a lot of choice. She only owned three dresses.

Friday morning after Dad and the boys left the house, Callie brought a tub into the kitchen and took a bath and washed her hair. She put on her best dress, the green one with little white stars printed all over it. In an effort to enhance it, she tied a wide white ribbon sash around her waist.

"Would you like me to fix your hair?"

Clem's offer surprised Callie, but she didn't hesitate to accept it. She wanted to improve her relationship with her sister if she could.

"Trace will like this," Clem assured Callie as she pulled the strands back and up on the sides. She worked the back of it into a fashionable arrangement of waves and curls held in place with hairpins.

When she finished, Clem handed Callie a mirror. Callie sat on the edge of the bed and tipped her head side to side to see what Clem had done—and couldn't believe her eyes. She couldn't go like this. It implied too much, that she would go to so much extra trouble for an outing with Trace. He might interpret it wrong.

She reached up to pull out the pins, but the sound of a motor outside brought her to a heart-thumping halt. Trace had arrived. There was no time to redo anything.

Callie lowered her hand and pressed it to her chest for a moment before going to the door. Trace stood on the step, hand raised to knock. Her heart rate tripled. He looked way too handsome in khaki pants and a dark blue shirt. His chocolate-brown hair had been combed back, but a strand with a mind of its own angled across his forehead.

He stepped inside and greeted her mother and Clem with a charming smile.

"I just have to get my purse," Callie managed to say. She ran to the bedroom and scooped it, along with a sweater, from the foot of the bed. When she returned, he placed a hand beneath her elbow and escorted her out the door and to his truck, his touch causing warmth to snake through her.

He steered her around to the driver's side of his truck and handed her the keys. "You've been driving on the country roads. Now that you have a license, it's time for you to drive in town."

So that's why he had taken her to get one weeks ago, before going to see Jolene one day after school.

Callie couldn't help but smile at his way of manipulating—and pleasing—her. "Are you sure you want to live that dangerously?"

"Yep." He went around to get in the passenger's side.

The miles passed way too quickly. Callie felt as if all her dreams were coming to life. Driving a vehicle instead of walking. In company with a handsome man who made her have thoughts of love—dreams she should not have. He was just a friend. She had to remember that.

Texas County had been named after the state of Texas, so it made perfect sense that they had given the name of Houston to the county seat town. When she pulled in and parked in front of the courthouse, Trace took the large envelope from the floorboard and got out. He leaned inside the door. "It won't take but a few minutes to get this recorded. Do you want to go in?"

She shook her head. "I'll wait for you here."

As he walked away, she leaned back and studied the area. Several automobiles occupied the streets, and three people strolled up the sidewalk ahead of Trace into the building. He was back beside her within ten minutes. "Okay, now let's relax and enjoy the afternoon."

She hesitated. "Where did you plan to go?"

He shrugged. "Wherever our impulses take us. Head back toward Deer Lick and take any side roads that you want to explore."

Callie started the truck and backed out. When she got out of town, she drove slower so they could pay more attention to the fall colors that highlighted the roadside and the distant Ozark ridges.

"It's incredible," she breathed in near-reverence.

"This has to be one of the most beautiful places God ever created."

His smile of agreement caused fresh tides of warmth to wash over her. She jerked her head back around and focused on the road.

As they got closer to Deer Lick, a side road caught Callie's eye. She turned onto it and drove even slower. They passed a farmhouse, then another one. Orange-dotted pumpkin patches had replaced gardens. On one farm two men picked corn in the crisp cool weather.

"I don't see how anyone can see all this, or human life, and deny the existence of God."

"Me, either," Callie responded. "But I admit that I sometimes have questions."

He turned in the seat and placed an arm along the top of it. "What kind of questions?"

She kept her eyes on the gravel road and drew a deep breath. "Why does God let life be so hard? Why does the country have to be in such an economic mess?"

"Maybe it's to make us more understanding of the desperate conditions in poorer countries. Or maybe it's to make us recognize that we should find joy in God's grace and mercy rather than in our goods and money."

She considered his words. "I can't fathom the mind of God, but I know that the church and individuals have to care for those who are hurting."

He nodded. "I know you take that seriously, and I admire how you reach out to others. I've become more conscious of the needs around us because of you."

Such a personal comment made Callie uneasy. "Community involvement is all right, but I'm learning that we shouldn't get so busy doing good that we don't spend time getting to know God better. Sometimes I have to be reminded of that."

The silence lingered for a moment too long before he broke it. "Does it bother you that your family doesn't have much?"

"You mean that we're poor?" she responded, unable to prevent a defensive tone.

"Okay, poor. Does it bother you?"

Her jaw tightened. So did her hands on the wheel. "Well, of course. Being poor is hard. Today, more people than ever know that. But some people seem to think that if you're poor, you're also dumb and worthless. They look down on you and make fun of you."

He seemed to absorb her resentment-tinged words. "I may have more money than you, but I sure don't think you're dumb. And I think you're worth a whole lot more than some I could name. I wish you and your family had more."

Callie heaved a drawn-out sigh, slowing the truck even more.

"Money, or the lack of it, puts a barrier between people."

"I don't feel any barrier between us. Do you?"

She had to be honest. "Some. Our lives have been very different. I've always been poor, and you've always had plenty."

"There's no shame in being poor. It's made you strong. Didn't Jesus make a point of ministering to the poor?"

"Yeah, yeah," she retorted. "The word *poor* could apply not only to those of low economic status, but also to those who are bound by spiritual poverty. But poverty is still hard. It's hard work and hard circumstances."

"Just don't let it come between us. Okay?"

She glanced over at him again. "We'll see."

"Turn here."

Surprised at the abrupt change in subject, Callie steered right at the fork in the road. They had circled around until they were within a mile of town.

"Pull in here."

She drove into what looked like a private lane. "How far should I go?"

He pointed ahead to a clearing. "Park in there."

Callie did as directed and leaned forward on the steering wheel. The field before them had a border of oaks and evergreens at the back of it. Her lips curved in a smile. "This is a pretty piece of property. Who owns it?"

"Me."

She turned her head quickly, and found it hard to get enough air into her lungs.

"Is this where you planned to live with Joanna?" Her voice came out slightly shaky.

He nodded. "We were going to live in town at first. But I planned to build a house out here when I could." His eyes stayed on her face as he spoke. "After her death I dropped all those plans. Lately I've been thinking about them again."

Callie didn't know what to say.

"Let's walk." He got out and came around to meet her as she stepped from the truck. She nearly forgot to breathe when he reached over and took her hand. She let him lead her along a faint trail worn in the grass by wildlife.

For several minutes they simply walked without talking, his hand around hers making her near-dizzy. Callie inhaled the crisp autumn air and hoped he couldn't tell how unsteady she felt.

He stopped beside a small creek and faced her. "I really like your hair."

She swallowed. "Clem did it. She likes to fuss with hair. It's a bit too fancy, but I couldn't…"

"Hurt her feelings?" He grinned. "I'm glad you couldn't. It suits you. I think you should let Clem fuss with your hair any time she wants."

Callie didn't resist—she couldn't—when he pulled her close to his chest. Her heart beat faster as he placed a hand at her nape and brought her face toward his. As if she had no will of her own, she moved her arms up around his neck and welcomed the warmth of his breath on her cheek, and then his lips so soft on hers. She melted against him as his mouth moved from her lips and trailed tender kisses over her face.

Was this how it felt to be in love? Even in her fairy-tale dreams she had never imagined such a feeling.

With her heart pounding, Callie eased back to where she could look up into his face. She blinked at the tenderness she read there. Neither of them spoke for long seconds.

"You're special, Callie." His voice came out husky.

"I'm not," she denied. "I'm an ordinary country girl without an asset to her name and no training for anything but ordinary hard work."

"You're warm and caring, unaffected and full of integrity. And I enjoy being with you."

She stepped back from him ever so slightly. "I…think we should go."

"How about we go find something to eat? Are you hungry?"

She stared at the small squint lines at the ends of his

eyes, having trouble putting her body into motion. "I think I could eat a horse."

A laugh rumbled up from his chest, and he placed a hand behind her waist. "Then let's go find a horse."

"Do you have a horse on the menu?" Trace asked when a young waitress approached. "We're hungry enough to eat one."

The young woman laughed. "Not today, but if you'll make a reservation for next Friday I'll do my best to have one."

Callie giggled at their silliness and began to relax.

They ordered the rib special, with corn on the cob and potatoes. When the waitress left, Trace reached over and took one of Callie's hands in his own. He offered a brief blessing.

It warmed Callie that he would pray in public. The fact that he also held her hand while doing so gave her the sense that he was strong, dependable and trustworthy, because he trusted and relied on God.

"I'm sorry about what happened to the man who shot Riley and Delmer," she said during a break in their comfortable conversation, and then wished she hadn't brought up that subject.

"I'm glad you're safe," he said simply. "A side benefit is that you won't have to testify against him in court."

She hadn't thought much about that aspect. "I wish the whole thing hadn't happened."

He leaned forward on his elbows. "But then you wouldn't have come home. I won't say I'm glad for any of the bad things that have happened, but I'm happy you're here."

Callie felt her face flush.

After he finished his piece of chocolate pie, Trace leaned back and watched while she worked on hers. "It's good to see you enjoy that."

She hesitated before taking the last bite. "They have a good cook here. She should be complimented."

"I'll take care of that when we check out. Will you go to the picture show with me before I take you home?"

This wasn't fair. How could she turn him down when all she wanted was to be with him? And a picture show would be exciting. "Okay," was all she could say.

He smiled in satisfaction.

Sprinkles of rain were falling when they exited the restaurant. Callie thought her heart would pound a hole in her chest when Trace took her hand and led her down Main Street. He released it to reach for his wallet as they walked up the two concrete steps onto the wide flat surface in front of the ticket booth.

To each side of the lighted area was a large framed sheet of glass with a big poster behind it. The one on the left advertised that *Our Gang* was showing tonight. The poster on the right showed that a popular swashbuckler would play Monday, Tuesday and Wednesday.

Trace bought tickets, and they went inside the lobby where the smell of popcorn greeted them. "Wait here." He stopped beside the door. "We can't watch a movie without popcorn."

"But we just ate," she protested.

He paused and gave her a crooked grin. "But it's a movie. You have to have popcorn."

She waved him away. "Oh, all right."

Callie watched people trickle in from outside and go inside the theater as she waited. Trace returned with a tray that held two sodas and two bags of popcorn. "Lead the way."

They found seats near the back just as Mickey Mouse appeared on the screen. Trace handed Callie a bag of popcorn and whispered in her ear. "The guy who created that character is from Missouri."

She nodded and took the sack without taking her eyes from the screen, afraid to reveal the way her heart fluttered from the feel of his breath on her cheek. She had heard how Walt Disney was making a name for himself with these animated films.

When he put his soda on the floor and placed his arm across the back of the seat behind her, she tried to ignore it. But when he gave her shoulder a light squeeze, she nearly fainted from the visions of happily ever after that floated before her eyes.

Stop being silly. This is simply a day in time. Nothing more can come of it.

Callie pushed the impossible dreams away. Only when he removed his arm to pick up his soda did she regain something close to normal breathing.

After the cartoon they watched two episodes of a group of poor children known as *Our Gang* outsmart rich-kid adversaries. Callie enjoyed it. But that wasn't the reason her heart made an extra thump every time Trace's arm touched hers.

"I loved it," she said as they exited the building, so happy she could have skipped all the way home, even though the skies had turned darker and sprinkles of rain continued to fall. They sprinted back up the street to the truck, where Trace still insisted she drive.

"You need the practice, and I need to monitor you." His voice was teasing.

Callie started the truck and drove out of town. She trembled inwardly as Trace watched her from the passenger seat, the look on his face making her wonder if he planned to kiss her again.

Soon after she turned off the highway onto the gravel road, the wind began to whip furiously around them, bending the field grass and tree limbs into eerie shadows. She gripped the wheel tighter and leaned forward to peer at the road in the beam of the headlights. She began to breathe easier as they started down the last hill within sight of her home.

Suddenly a huge black form sprang from the ditch into the road ahead of them.

Chapter 12

Just as Callie identified the form as a cow, probably cantankerous old Bossy, the animal lurched forward into the road.

In a desperate effort to avoid hitting it, she jerked the wheel to the left. The fender grazed the cow, and the animal darted back toward the ditch, but the truck skidded the opposite direction. As Callie tried to regain control, the left tires hit loose gravel and the truck careened into the ditch. They landed with a thud that snapped Callie's head forward onto the steering wheel with a crack. Trace was thrown against her.

He reached over and turned off the motor. "Are you all right?"

Stunned and disoriented, Callie raised her head and fought blackness. The world spun and eddied around her for several moments. Horror seeped through her as she comprehended what had happened. Her eyes teared, and her hands covered her mouth. "Your truck," she moaned.

"Don't worry about the truck." Trace ran a hand over her forehead. "Are you hurt? I hope I didn't squash you."

She rolled her head back against the seat. "I'm okay. But I've wrecked your truck. I've smashed it, and we'll never push it out of this ditch. I'm so sorry." Her voice rose to a wail.

"It's not your fault, Callie." He pulled her to him. It was an awkward position with them both practically lodged beneath the steering wheel. "Just sit still and let your head clear."

Too dizzy to argue, Callie let her head loll against his shoulder and fought to control her lurching stomach. As the world gradually righted and the blackness cleared, she became aware of the wind still whipping around the truck in the dark. The truck practically lay on the driver's side, up against the side of the ditch. They would have to climb out on the passenger's side.

She forced her eyes open and tried to ease away from Trace. But they were wedged in tight. She heard him chuckle and felt his chest vibrate.

"At least I got to hold you again. Will it hurt your head too much if I blow the horn?"

She frowned, slow to understand.

"We're close enough to your house that someone should hear it and come help us."

"If the guys aren't still down at the barn, they should hear us. But if they had to go back and finish chores after supper, they might not." Slowly regaining her senses, Callie reached up and pressed the horn herself. The loud bleep rang in her brain as she held it down.

When she couldn't stand the noise any longer, Callie released the horn.

Trace looked over at the passenger door. "If I can raise that door and get out, I'll pull you out after me. Just sit tight." Using the steering wheel and dashboard for leverage, he eased his way to his knees on the seat and pushed the door upward. He was trying to figure out a way to keep it from falling shut when they heard shouts from up the road.

Barely visible behind the beam of a flashlight, two figures came toward them.

"It's my brothers."

Trace eased the door down. Moments later it was pulled open from the outside. Hands reached inside. "Let's get you out of there," Riley's voice said.

"I'll have to come first." Trace sounded reluctant, but he was between Callie and the door. He let Riley and Delmer hoist him out. Then he leaned in and extended both hands to Callie. "Come on, pretty girl. Let me pull you up."

Callie ignored the endearment and pushed herself past the steering wheel. She reached up, and he grasped one of her hands firmly in each of his. Moments later she climbed over the running board and jumped to the road.

"We met Bossy back there," Delmer said. "Did she cause this?"

Trace gave a good-natured chuckle. "There was a cow, but she didn't give me her name."

Riley knelt on the roadside and swung a flashlight beam underneath the truck. "I think you should leave this here until daylight so we can see to check the damage. If it's all right, we'll pull it out with the horses."

"We'll take you home in the buckboard," Delmer added.

Trace took Callie's hand. "Sounds like they know best."

The four of them set out walking the short distance to the house, Riley pointing the way with his flashlight. Trace turned off his flashlight and gave Callie's hand a secret squeeze that made her feel cherished.

"We'll hitch up the team and be right back," Riley said when they entered the yard. The house was dark. The Blake family went to bed early and got up before dawn. "You stay here and keep Callie company, town boy." He and Delmer disappeared into the dark.

Trace chuckled. "I've been put in my place."

"You don't sound upset."

He steered her over by the gate and closed the space between them. "We should take advantage of these few minutes alone. I'm sure they expect it of us."

Callie leaned into him as his mouth covered hers in a gentle kiss that made her legs go weak. He raised his head and ran a palm over the curve of her cheek. Then he grazed his lips over hers once more. "You should go on in now, or I'll keep doing this," he whispered in her ear. "I'll be back for the truck in the morning."

"I'm sorry…"

A finger came across her lips, silencing her. "Don't worry about it. The same thing would have happened if I had been driving."

Callie edged away and started toward the house. When she reached the doorway, she looked back at him. He waved from the gate. "Good night, Callie."

Hearing her brothers returning, she turned and went inside.

Callie listened from inside the door as the buckboard rolled away. Then she got ready for bed. She stared up at the ceiling as a haze of moonbeams glimmered through the window and gave the room an eerie light. Her emotions ran hot and cold.

Trace's face floated in her mind—handsome and lean, those intense blue eyes and ready smile—and brought familiar warmth through her entire being. But worrisome thoughts followed.

I've damaged his truck. He made light of it, and I'm sure my savings would not be enough to fix it.

Callie shifted from her back to her stomach. Then back again.

"Be quiet over there. I'm trying to sleep."

Clem's growl from the next bed made Callie go rigid and silent. She closed her eyes and willed herself to sleep. Whispering a prayer for wisdom, she slipped into a fragmented slumber. And woke before daylight to the sounds of creaking harnesses and plodding hooves.

She had no idea how Riley and Delmer had managed to leave the house without waking her, but they had hitched the team and were headed to Trace's truck. Which meant he must be out there. She glanced over and saw the shadow of Clem's form still in bed.

Callie grabbed her robe from the foot of the bed, slipped her feet into her shoes and hurried to the kitchen and out the back door. Clutching the robe to her, she made a quick trip to the outhouse, scanning the yard and road for her brothers and Trace. She spotted the three of them hunkered down on the roadway, peering under Trace's truck, apparently trying to hook it to the singletree positioned behind the horses.

She resumed her trek and then hurried back to the

kitchen where Mom now puttered around starting breakfast. Callie brushed her teeth and gathered two jars of pickles and a bag of squash. "Mom, will you have Clem bring these when she comes to the swap meet? I'm going on ahead to help Jolene get the room ready."

Mom frowned at her. "You're not going without breakfast, are you?"

Callie reached into the cabinet and grabbed a cold biscuit. "I'll eat this on the way."

She hurried back to the bedroom and scrambled into her blue dress that happened to be clean. Then she ducked out the back door, ignoring her mother's questioning look.

Walking briskly, Callie circled around behind the barn and cut across the woods past her frog pond. She circled around the place in the road where Trace and her brothers were working with the truck, and emerged onto the main road.

When she got to the turnoff to the Delaney farm she stopped to get her breath. As she had hoped, Jolene came driving up the lane five minutes later. She stopped and rolled down a window. "Hop in."

Callie slid into the passenger seat and studied her friend's appearance. She looked tired, but the color in her face had improved. "How are things going with you?"

Jolene shrugged and pulled onto the road. "We're learning to live without Mother, but missing her like crazy. Going back to school has been good for me because it keeps me too busy to mope. Irene seems to be doing all right, but she keeps so much to herself that it's hard to tell how she's really feeling."

"Being back in school and around children her age has to be good for her," Callie said.

Jolene sighed and rubbed a palm across the steering

wheel. "She's a good kid. Almost too good. Mother was sick so much that Irene grew up too fast."

"She was fortunate to have you." Callie reached over and gave Jolene's hand a squeeze. "I know you'll continue to be more of a mother than a sister to her. If you ever need someone to keep her so you can spend more time at school, or you just need a break, please let me do it."

Jolene gave her a sad look. "Thanks. I'll do that." Then a bit of a smile crept over her face. "Are you and Trace Gentry getting serious?"

Taken off guard, Callie's mouth opened and closed, but no sound came out.

Jolene made a right turn into the area behind the car dealership. She parked and faced Callie across the seat. "He's shown a lot of interest in you, and you deserve a good man."

"He's a good friend." Callie shook her head, her voice catching.

"I see." Jolene nodded as if she had just figured out the secret of the universe. "I think you care more about him than you're willing to admit, even to yourself."

Callie hauled in a huge breath and let it out in a rush. "Maybe I do. But it can't come to anything."

Jolene's eyes narrowed. "Why not? He's a good catch. So are you. And people have noticed you together."

Callie gave an unladylike snort. This conversation was getting way too uncomfortable. "I'm sure they have."

What's going through that girl's mind?

Trace hit the brake too hard as he pulled in behind the building, hanging on to the handle of the damaged driver's door to keep it from flying open. He sat for a moment, taking in the number of cars and wagons parked there.

"This is a good thing they're doing here," he muttered, as if convincing himself. Memories of last night's kiss caused images of Callie's lips to mingle with memories of Joanna. He was treading dangerous waters—and heedlessly moving deeper rather than heading for the shore.

Determined to find out why Callie had left so much earlier than Riley said she normally did and was already gone when he went to get her, he slid from the truck seat and stalked toward the building. At the door he paused to compose himself. Calmer, he went inside. It only took a moment to spot her, looking as appealing as ever. When she glanced up and saw him, she suddenly became very busy. He pretended he didn't recognize the avoidance and marched toward her.

He stopped before her table and watched her push items around on it. "Callie, why didn't you wait? I would have given you a ride to town."

She raised her head, but looked more at his shoulder than right at him. "I needed to get here early, and you had to get your truck out of a ditch and fixed. Which I *will* pay for."

So that was it. She insisted on taking responsibility, and she didn't have the money to do it. "Callie, I told you not to worry about it. It was an accident. Like I figured, there wasn't much damage, just a flat tire and a sprung door. I can fix all that myself."

She faced him directly now, as if gauging his honesty. "Okay, so you can fix the door. But you'll need a new tire. Get one and charge it to me."

"I will not." He spoke in an exasperated huff. "I'll fix the one I have."

"Now that gardens are finished, we're only going to do this every other Saturday."

He nodded, interpreting her change of subject as acceptance. "That makes sense. I'll put a sign on the door, and I assume Jolene will put the information in the newspaper."

"That sounds good."

"How about we go out to my brother's later this week and pitch some horseshoes with him and his wife. They have friends over every Friday evening, and they're always asking me to come and bring someone with me."

She frowned. "I need to stay closer to home. My mother counts on me."

He shifted his feet, wishing he could hug her and reassure her. "What about you? Don't you think it's time to consider your own needs and wants? Do you plan to spend the rest of your life taking care of them?"

She shrugged. "It's my life, how it's always been."

"Don't you ever plan to marry, have a family of your own?"

She released a startled gasp. "I can't think about such a thing right now. I have too much to do here."

He reached over and gripped her arm. "At least go to dinner with me, just the two of us." He had never had to pressure a girl to see him, and couldn't believe he was doing it now.

She pushed his hand away and stepped back. "I can't, Trace." She headed toward Jolene, as if running from herself.

Monday evening at the end of supper, Riley pushed back his chair and got up. "I'm going out to split some more wood while there's still a little light."

Callie bounced to her feet. "I'll help you." Clem could do the dishes.

She got her coat and followed him out the kitchen door to the lower edge of the backyard where a mallet and an ax leaned against a tree. A woodpile about four feet high stretched between that tree and another one almost eight feet from it.

Riley picked up the maul and swung it with one hand at the wedge he held in place with the other hand. Callie watched him work, happy to have him back to his normal, strong self. He had always been her protector and confidant. Taller than Delmer, he had an engaging smile that didn't get used nearly enough, and he loved to tease her. She wondered if he stayed single because the folks needed him, or whether there could be other reasons.

"What's on your mind?" Riley asked as she gathered an armload of the pieces.

He knew her too well. "I don't get a chance to spend much time alone with you."

He propped the ax upright against a chunk of log. "Yeah, but you followed me out here in a hurry. I think there's more on your mind."

She bit her lip, unsure how to ask. "Well, I was kind of wondering if you might have any idea how I could even things up with Trace."

He frowned. "I don't follow you."

"I feel bad about his truck. I was driving it, so I think I should pay for the damage. But he says it's not hurt much and for me to forget it."

"But you can't, huh?"

She shook her head. "Is the damage as little as he makes out?"

Riley rubbed his chin. "It didn't look bad. The door's sprung enough he has to hold it shut while driving, but he says he can fix it. And we had to take off a flat tire and put on his spare."

Callie trusted Riley. That agreed with what Trace had said. She breathed easier.

"You like him a lot, don't you?"

Callie became evasive. "Everyone likes him."

"Sure, they do, but not in the way we both know I'm talking about. From what I've seen, he likes you just as much. And both of you deserve to find someone special. You have my approval." He grinned with mischief. "Which you must have if you plan to pair up with him."

She swatted at him. "Stop spouting nonsense. Trace and I are good friends, is all."

"Yeah, yeah, if you say so." His face lost its teasing look. "You want to do something for him, don't you? You feel beholden, even if you shouldn't."

"Yes."

He looked upward, as if he could find ideas in the stars that were beginning to dot the sky. "I know you have a little savings meant for a car. I also know he would never take it. So what could he use that we could give him?"

"He owns a piece of property that he planned to build a house on after he and Joanna got married."

Riley snapped his fingers. "That's it. If he had the lumber, he could build a house. We cut timber and make lumber. You're the one who believes in swapping things. We'll cut some extra lumber and take him a load. Delmer will help. It won't build a house, bit it'll give him a start if he wants it."

Callie's face broke into a grin. "That's a good idea." Then her countenance fell. "But you and Delmer don't have time to cut an extra load."

Riley went solemn. He hesitated, as if unsure how

much to say. "We're not all that busy anymore. No one has any money to order lumber. I think Dad's worried. I've tried talking to him, but he won't tell me how bad things are."

A knot of tension formed in Callie's gut.

They worked for a few more minutes. Then Riley stopped. "It's too dark to do any more. You go on inside, and I'll be in after I put this ax away."

Callie started to leave, but stopped. "Riley, you have my approval if you want to court Jolene. You'd like to, wouldn't you?"

"What I'd like and what's possible aren't the same. Now, get in the house before I tan your hide for meddling."

Callie wished she could see his face clearly, but it was too dark. "You and who else?" she teased, backing away. Then she turned and ran for the house.

Over the next two weeks Callie concluded that Riley was right. Her parents were tight-lipped and evasive. They refused to answer questions about anything other than daily routine.

Watching the growing number of worry lines in her parents' faces, their lack of talkativeness and unsmiling expressions had her a nervous wreck. She dreaded knowing the truth, but by Thursday she couldn't stand it any longer. She waited until Dad and her brothers went back to work after lunch, and Clem took the slop bucket to the barn to feed the pigs.

"How bad is it, Mom?"

Dessie just shook her head and didn't speak. Her mouth tightened and quivered.

"I have to know, Mom. We're all affected. What kind of money trouble are we in?"

Mom's lips trembled. "It's…pretty bad," she choked.

Callie took her mother's hands and guided her down onto a chair. Then she sat in the one facing her. "Tell me. We all have to know if we're going to help."

A tear trickled down Mom's cheek. She made a quick swipe at it. Then she took a deep breath. "We're losing everything."

Callie wrapped an arm around her shoulders. "How? Why? Explain it to me. Riley said business isn't good. What else is wrong?"

Mom took a deep, shuddering breath and began to speak in a tremulous voice. "A few months before the crash, Arlie borrowed money against the house to buy the tractor and replace the old wood-powered steam engine with the new gas-powered one. Business wuz good when he did it, and we had no trouble making the payments. But we've missed the past two, and the bank is going to foreclose on us. I don't know what we're going to do."

Callie felt as if she had been punched in the gut. She searched for words, for strength. "You've always taught us to seek help from God when we're in trouble. I'll admit I'm a little shaky in that area right now. But I think it's time to talk to Him."

Mom's shoulders shuddered, and she nodded. They clasped hands and bowed their heads.

"Lord, we're in trouble and need Your help here. Please show us what to do."

When Callie stopped, Mom cleared her throat and began to pray. "Father, Callie's right. We have to trust You. We gotta have a place to live, and we need Your help to not lose it. Please help us. Amen."

Mom went back to her kitchen cleanup, but Callie went to the bedroom and began to search for guidance in her

Bible. The preacher always said that when all they had was God, they had all they needed. She needed more reassurance, though.

Luke 13:7 reminded her that nothing is impossible with God. Then she moved farther over in the book of Luke and began to read the parable about the rich man who would pull down his barns and build bigger ones to store his goods, and was called a fool for laying up earthly treasures rather than being rich with God. She read on.

And seek not what ye shall eat or what ye shall drink, neither be ye of doubtful mind. For all these things do the nations of the world seek after: and your Father knoweth that ye have need of these things. But rather seek ye the kingdom of God; and all these things shall be added unto you. Fear not, little flock; for it is your Father's good pleasure to give you the kingdom.

She put the Bible down and spent some time on her knees. Then she went back to work, resolved to trust God, whatever He had in store for them.

Chapter 13

On Saturday afternoon Trace answered a knock at his door and found Riley Blake standing there, twisting a battered hat in his hands.

"We took a load of lumber out to a piece of property Callie says you own."

Trace's jaw dropped at the words. He stared at Riley's thick black hair that could use a trim, still amazed at how much he resembled Callie. "Why did you do that?"

"Callie wanted to do something for you."

Now he understood. "Your sister is one stubborn gal," he said in a huff. "What does she expect me to do with it?"

A boyish grin tugged at Riley's mouth, transforming him. "She says you once planned to build a house out there, and she thought it could give you a bit of a start if you ever decide to take up your plans again."

"She's determined to replace that tire, isn't she?" He shook his head in exasperation.

God resisteth the proud, but giveth grace unto the humble.

These people humbled him. They had little, yet they shared what they did have. *Lord, forgive me for my prideful and selfish ways.*

Riley nodded and grinned, and then he became serious. "She's a good girl. And I wouldn't want to see anyone ever hurt her or mistreat her."

A threat? Not exactly. But a warning from a protective older brother. Trace got it.

"She is a good girl," he agreed.

"She tries to take care of everyone," Riley continued. "Someday I hope someone takes care of her." He turned to go.

"If someone wanted to take care of her, would he need your approval?"

Riley turned back. "He might." But his mouth held a suspicious quirk. He turned again and walked away.

As he watched Riley go to the street and climb onto the horse he had left tethered to the gatepost, Trace's mind spun. He suspected he had just been given the go-ahead to pursue Callie, and he thought he might have a glimmer of how to go about it. She may have refused to go out with him, but she couldn't turn down a request to help someone in need.

All day Monday Callie wrestled with what to do. Her parents needed money desperately, and they needed it now. Oblivious to the chilly weather and overcast sky, she came to a decision—and gave up her dreams.

Tuesday morning she helped Mom and Clem clean up

from breakfast. Then she changed into her best dress, a
navy blue one with a white collar and cuffs, pinned her
hair back into a bun and put on her coat. She picked up
her purse, which contained her savings that she had removed from its hiding place before going to bed the night
before, and left the house.

All the way to town she prayed, sometimes silently,
sometimes aloud. "Lord, direct my path. Help us all."

When she got to town, she marched up the street and
into the bank. A teller greeted her with a smile. "May I
help you?"

"I need to talk to the person in charge of loans."

"Oh, you want to take out a loan?"

"No, I want to make payments on one."

Thirty minutes later she exited the bank and drew a
deep breath. She no longer had any savings, but her parents' two missed payments were no more. She considered going into the drugstore for a cold drink, but decided
against it. She only had two dollars left to her name.

The trek home took longer. *What next, Lord?*

Callie could see only one option. She had to leave
again, go where she could find work.

That evening after supper she joined Riley at the
woodpile again. The temperature had dropped below
forty, and a breeze whispering through the trees made
the evening feel a bit eerie.

They worked in silence until it got too dark to see.

"You act guilty," Riley said as she picked up the last
of the wood.

Callie couldn't see his face, but she could hear a smile
in his voice. She hated to spoil his good mood. "I asked
Mom point-blank about their finances. She admitted

they've missed the past two payments on the loan they took out over a year ago."

He put the wood down and sat on an upturned chunk of log. "Sit and tell me about it."

Callie sat, but she hesitated to speak.

"I know you went to town this morning. What did you do?"

"I robbed the bank and made those payments," she said in a rush.

He chuckled. "Okay, the law hasn't come for you. So how did you pay them?"

She explained about her savings.

He ran a hand over his face. "Callie, I know how much of a sacrifice that was for you, how much you've wanted for so long to buy a car. But I'm sure they appreciate it." He paused. "If they know. Do they?"

She shook her head, and then realized he probably couldn't see the motion. "No, and you can't tell them. They'll find out from the bank soon enough."

He went silent for long seconds. Then his voice penetrated the darkness. "You're getting ready to take off, aren't you?"

"I don't see any choice. That only catches up what they missed. Another payment will be due before long. I have to find a paying job."

He heaved an audible sigh. "Will you at least try to find something around here first? Having you back home makes the folks happy. And they'll be hurt if you leave again just so you can help them."

She did a mental check of places to look for a job. "I'll go back to town tomorrow."

"Good. Let's go in and have a cup of hot coffee. I'm chilled."

* * *

Wednesday morning after breakfast Callie set out for town again.

Once inside the city limits she worked her way up one side of the street and down the other, entering each business and asking whether they needed to hire any help. The answers were worded differently, but the result was the same at each. No one needed, or could afford, help. Some were releasing workers they already had.

Time ran out and businesses began to close before she could get to those on the outskirts of town, so she went home.

Callie didn't sleep that night. She got up Thursday morning and went back to town. No one needed help—none that they had to pay for, anyhow.

"Whoa." The sight of Trace knocked the wind from her as he gripped her arms to steady her. "Where are you headed in such a hurry? And all dressed up, too." He ran an appreciative eye over her.

Why did she have to lose her calm every time she saw him? She backed away. "I was thinking and not watching where I was going."

"You real busy, or just out for a stroll?"

Callie didn't want to explain and end up blabbing her personal problems to him. "Running errands." Well, she was.

He released her arms and flicked a stray strand of hair back from her face. "So am I. Would you have time to help me with one?"

She tipped her head and frowned up at him. "What kind of errand?"

"First, let me thank you for the lumber. It wasn't necessary, but it's appreciated. I guess I can understand your need to do something."

"It isn't enough to do a lot, but it could make a start on something of your own."

He gave a crooked grin. "Like a house? Are you saying you think I should build one?"

She shrugged. "I can't imagine you being happy without your own place indefinitely."

"You're probably right. I've—"

"What's the errand you need help with?" she cut him off, uncomfortable at the images floating through her mind. Trace in a home of his own—with a family.

"Your lumber reminded me that Joanna's parents aren't well and can't keep enough wood cut for their needs. I have a load piled behind the dealership that I planned to take to them. Do you have time to run out there with me?"

She pierced him with narrowed eyes. Doubts raged inside her. "You don't need my help."

"Yes, I do," he insisted. "I have to load it in my truck, and I'm sure Mrs. Michaels would love a chance to visit with another woman."

Her eyes brightened with understanding. "Ah, so what you really want is company for her. All right. I've accomplished all I can this afternoon."

Which was absolutely nothing.

He took her hand. "Let's go."

Callie knew as soon as they set out that she had made a mistake. She couldn't be around Trace and not have dreams start forming in her head, dreams that could never be. Especially now.

It didn't take long to load the wood. Callie refused

Trace's invitation to drive the newly repaired truck and eased into the passenger seat.

She stiffened her shoulders in resolve. Trace was everything she could want in a man—if she were free to consider a relationship with one. But she had a family in need. Courting was the last thing on her mind. She had to find a paying job.

They found the Michaels house quiet and deserted. So they stacked the wood neatly against the fence. "I'll take you home," he said when they finished.

Callie brushed her hands. "That's not necessary. My feet are in perfect working order."

He cocked his head at an angle. "I know that. Does it never occur to you that I might want to spend time with you?"

It did. That's what scared her. She couldn't let herself love him and walk away. Yet she was too spineless to turn down a ride home. It would save her time and energy, she justified to herself as she got back in the truck.

Trace started the engine. To Callie's surprise, he drove in silence. Just before getting to her house, Trace turned left into the now-deserted school yard. She frowned over at him in question.

He didn't speak until he had parked next to the school building and turned off the motor. He turned in the seat to face her. "Let's chat."

She scooted back against the door. "I don't know anything to talk about."

"Sure you do. Tell me what's in that head of yours. Just tell me about yourself."

"It's boring stuff."

"Not to me. I'm interested in everything about you."

She was sure that those deep-set blue eyes could see

right through her. He held her gaze, making her want to crawl across that seat and snuggle up into the curve of his arm, feel the warmth he could create in her.

The sight of leaves borne on the wind past them broke her line of thought. "Is this supposed to be a two-way flow of information?"

He shrugged. "If you'd like. I have no secrets."

Of course, that didn't mean that everyone in the community knew how his mind worked, what thoughts he harbored. Callie wished she did.

"Friends share their lives, their thoughts."

He considered them friends. Just friends. Okay, she could push her deeper feelings aside and handle that. She drew a deep breath and exhaled slowly. "Okay."

He leaned back against the truck door. "Did you have a hard time when you were little?"

Hard time. He didn't know the half of it. She squinted at him. "You know I did. We did."

"Your family."

She nodded and tried to keep from wiggling in the seat. "I'm the fifth of seven children of very poor parents. It's a good thing I don't require much."

He chuckled. "I'm glad they didn't stop having children after the fourth. Did you grow up right here?" He nodded at the house across the road.

She shook her head. "My folks lived in Oklahoma before I was born. When Dad lost his job they moved back to Missouri. He hired a driver to bring Mom and the kids in a wagon, and he followed to drive the stock. Mom was expecting me, and she went to her stepbrother's to wait for Dad. I was born before he got here."

"Come here."

No. Don't go into his arms.

Callie watched Trace's hand pat the seat beside him.

And, like a moth to the flame, she scooted that way. When his arm curved around her shoulders and pulled her to him, she leaned into his chest, a buzz filtering through her brain.

He nestled her under his chin, nuzzled his face in her hair. "Go on with what you were saying."

Callie felt so sheltered, warm and safe. With a sigh of surrender, she melted against him.

"Dad bought a sawmill, and we lived on Water Hollow where he cut timber for other people," she continued falteringly. "Times were lean. I remember once when we didn't have anything to eat until Dad got back from town. Riley and I ate salt and drank water to keep us from being so hungry. When Dad came in from the store, Mom warmed some grease and poured milk in it and made grease gravy and pancakes. It tasted wonderful to me."

Trace didn't say anything, but his arms constricted around her.

Neither of them spoke for long moments. His breath brushed against her hair. "Did things ever get better?"

Callie plucked at her dress. "We moved to Deer Lick soon after that. We lived in a two-story house near Deer Creek. The steam engine was run by wood, and one day a spark from it blew on top of the house and set it on fire. It burned to the ground. At first we lived in a house on the highway and walked a mile and a half. Then we moved closer and started coming to Deer Creek School. Later Dad bought that forty acres of land."

She dipped her head to indicate across the road. "He built our house, and we've lived there ever since. The best thing about it to me was that we finally got to attend school regularly."

She stopped speaking. His pleasant male scent held her spellbound. It was different from the woodsy smells she associated with the men of her family, more tangy.

"If you could have anything you want, what would it be?"

Callie drew in a deep breath. "All I ever wanted for my family was to know we would have plenty of food to eat and be able to pay our bills. The only luxuries I've wanted for myself are a car…and a new dress that wasn't a hand-me-down or homemade," she added in a flash of honesty. "But those dreams have gotten farther away rather than closer."

"You saw no choice but to find work and help your family right after high school."

"No." Just like she didn't see a choice now.

"I'm glad you came back." He paused. "Surely you know that I care for you."

She drew back and placed a palm against his lips. "Please don't."

He gripped the hand and lowered it. "But why?"

She shook her head. "I have too many responsibilities to think about what it might mean."

His look of perplexity turned to a frown. "Are you telling me what I think it sounds like?"

She uttered a harsh half laugh, half sob. "Only if it sounds like goodbye."

He drew upright and removed his arm from around her. "Just like that? You're telling me you have to take care of your family and can't see me anymore?"

Callie had gone numb. She placed fingers over her lips to stop their quivering. Then she scooted to the passenger door. She looked back at him. "For what it's worth, I care for you, too. But I have to do what I have to do."

* * *

Cold that had nothing to do with the weather seeped through Trace as Callie opened the door and got out. He watched her cross the road and go inside her house. As the door closed, something closed inside him.

She had such simple dreams that they made him feel small for taking his life of comforts for granted. But she had shut him out. The thought of life without her made him ache. He had no choice, though. She had left him none. What could he do?

He would stay busy. The business needed his concentration. And his parents could probably benefit from a little more personal attention.

The time after Joanna's death had been dark. He tried to recall her face, but all that came to mind was Callie's dark eyes and sweet lips. Darkness enveloped him again.

Chapter 14

Springfield, Missouri
Five months later

Callie's feet hurt. Waitress work involved being on her feet all day. No sitting down to break beans or peel potatoes. She had to walk back and forth between the kitchen and hungry customers a zillion times. At least it seemed that many. But she thanked God every day that Ruby Palmer's restaurant drew a steady stream of customers.

Not only was she exhausted from a ten-hour shift, but her emotions were also at a low ebb. She was lonely. What she wouldn't give for a chance to see Trace, talk to him, feel his arms around her. A deep hole in her heart made her chest ache.

She trudged home in the bitter February cold. Rather, she trudged to Aunt Lily's small frame house she called home. She slipped into the house quietly, pasted a smile on her weary face and crossed the dark living room to the lighted kitchen.

Aunt Lily spun around, a hand pressed to her chest. "Mercy, I didn't hear you come in." Thin to the point of gauntness, Callie's aunt Lily radiated calm confidence and practiced a no-nonsense approach to life. She had married young, but lost her husband in an influenza epidemic a few months later. Grief stricken, she had lost the baby she carried. She had never remarried and lived the life of a spinster. She worked as a teller in a bank and lived a fairly comfortable life—especially for these times. She had welcomed Callie into her home in Springfield— hours away by buckboard—and insisted she stay there rather than rent a room. Callie had accepted the room, but insisted on paying rent. They got along fine.

"There's food in the warmer." Aunt Lily nodded toward the stove. "I went ahead and ate since you said you had to work late."

Callie shook her head. "I ate at the restaurant. I'm tired. If you don't mind, I'd like to clean up and go to bed."

The kind woman's face took on a sympathetic look. "Go ahead and get some rest. Oh, but let me give you your mail first. You have a letter from your friend."

Aunt Lily got up and went to the living room. Moments later she returned and handed Callie an envelope. She gave her a peck on the cheek. "You run on now."

Callie hurried to her little bedroom and took off her coat. She placed the letter on the bed and took her nightgown and robe to the bathroom across the hall, a wondrous luxury she prayed to have in a home of her own someday.

After her bath, she crawled into bed and propped herself up against the headboard with pillows. She opened the envelope and began to read.

Dear Callie,
I loved your last letter. Please write more often if you can.
I stop by after school a couple of times a week and check on your family. Clem is still helping me with the swap meets. We've only had them once a month these past two months, but we plan to go back to doing them every other week next month. Clem always brings her scissors and gives free haircuts when we do have them. I think she's staying home and helping your mother more.
Your parents miss you, especially your mother. She feels bad that you have to help them this way, but she accepts that it's the only way they can keep from losing their home. She says to tell you they're doing better, and the loan is getting close to being paid in full.

The passing weeks had brought a form of success for Callie, but nothing ceased the ache of loneliness in her heart. She sighed and nearly wept as she read the rest of Jolene's news about her own family, the school and how much she missed their times together.

Two days after arriving in Springfield, Callie had noticed a Help Wanted sign in the window of the restaurant a few blocks from the house, applied and been hired. A few weeks later she had stopped at the nearby car dealership—again. When she overheard one salesman telling another that he wished they had someone to keep their vehicles clean, she had told them she would do it, and been hired to wash cars on her days off from the restaurant. It didn't pay much, but it was money she could save toward buying a car. She sent her restaurant pay to her mother.

She missed her family. She missed the country, amid the noise and scramble of the city.

She missed Trace.

As the weeks passed, Trace missed Callie until he thought he would scream in agony. The end of something that had filled him with hope sank him to sadness akin to despair. The future once again held only emptiness. Anger ate at him like acid that she could walk away when he wanted her to stay so badly.

How bad was the Blake family situation? Should he find out more?

"You look like a man with a lot on his mind." Riley Blake greeted him with an inquisitive look when Trace approached the back of the field where Riley was shutting down the steam engine and putting away tools.

Trace eyed the pile of freshly cut boards a few yards from the machine. "Looks like you've been busy."

Riley snorted. "Too bad we don't have enough customers to keep us busier. What can I do for you? Or is it Dad you came to see?" He nodded at Arlie Blake on his way to the toolshed with an armload of tools.

"Got a few minutes you can spare?"

Being out here made it impossible for Trace to keep from remembering Callie in her overalls, plunking frogs in the pond beyond them. She belonged here, in the country, running free. It amazed him how at home he had come to feel out here. A fresh sense of abandonment filled him.

Lord, why did You let me fall in love with her and then let her leave me? How am I supposed to live without her?

Riley's throat clearing brought him back to attention. "What do you want?"

How could he ask?

"Well, I wondered if you would tell me more about why Callie…your sister left. I mean, I don't understand why she had to do it."

Riley's gaze raked him from head to foot, up and down and back again, as if he were a hog being examined for market readiness—or butchering. "Why do you want to know such personal stuff?"

"I miss her."

A hint of a twitch pulled at the corners of Riley's pursed mouth. "So do I. We all do."

"Couldn't she have stayed?" He felt like a beggar, pleading for crumbs of information.

Riley's body visibly relaxed. "The folks borrowed money they can't pay back. They missed a couple of payments, and the bank told them they would be foreclosing on the house. Callie made Mom tell her the truth. She paid the missed payments with her savings and tried to find work around here. She couldn't, so she went where she could."

Trace stilled his face through the dispassionate recital. He looked up at the sky as pain rocked him. "She loves her family."

"I think she would like to add to her family," Riley said with a lopsided near-smirk. "And I suspect you would be agreeable."

Trace turned his eyes back onto the wiry man. "I'd give her the moon if I could."

A finger went to Riley's mouth as he nodded. "I think

you would at that. Well, if you found out all you came for, I've got chores waiting. Come around again when we can catch some fish down at the pond."

A friendship with Riley Blake could be a good thing. It was something he could pursue. But for Callie, he could only wait.

He got back in the truck and glanced around the mill, his thoughts churning. He needed his own space. Was it time to resurrect his plans to build a house? If he went ahead now, would he have to live in it alone?

This could be a big mistake, but he had to take the risk. Making an on-the-spot decision, he got back out of the truck. "Hey, Riley," he called as Riley headed toward the toolshed.

Riley stopped and turned around. "You need something else?"

"I want to order some lumber."

Surprise lit Riley's face. He came back, and they met halfway. "How much, and when do you need it?"

"I want enough to build a house, minus one load."

Riley frowned. Then his face brightened. "Ah, the one we hauled out to your place."

Trace ignored the smug grin. "I want it in time to build a house in the spring. And I'll need a carpenter, maybe a couple of them. Do you do that kind of work?"

"Yep. Dad and us boys built that back when Delmer and me wuz just boys." He tipped his head in the direction of their house. "We've done a lot more of that kind of work since."

"Would you consider working for me?"

Riley scratched his head. "Hadn't thought about such a thing, but it sounds good. Business has been so slow that Dad and Delmer could probably get by without me here."

"If something came up and they needed you, we could work it out."

Riley considered for a moment, and then he smiled. "That would mean I could help the folks more with the bills, and maybe you could help Dad find that steal of a deal on a used car?" He phrased the last as a question.

Trace stuck out a hand. "When can you start?"

Riley shrugged. "Tomorrow soon enough?"

On his way back to his truck Trace felt good, like he had taken a step in the right direction.

"Ah…ah…ah…choo!"

No one sneezed like Aunt Lily. They came on in slow catches of breath, and then erupted from her with a loud force that jarred her entire body.

Callie grinned at the thin woman kneeling next to a flower bed among her bulbs, seeds and plants. She crossed the small yard toward her. "Aunt Lily, you need to go inside. This spring pollen is killing you."

The sky had cleared, the temperature had warmed and greenery sprang from the earth. The one downside of this entire coming-to-life process was the pollen that flooded the air.

"I habda ged my flowers in," her aunt said past swollen sinuses that affected her speech, the flower on her wide-brimmed straw hat jiggling as her head shook.

Callie put down the big bucket she carried and dropped to her knees beside the older woman. "Then let me help you so you can finish sooner." She reached for a dahlia bulb.

"At least you godda wash cars doday."

Callie laughed. "Some of them were almost solid yellow from pollen."

"You muss be dired." Aunt Lily eyed Callie's pollen-smeared and spattered overalls.

Callie shrugged and pulled a handful of weeds from the edge of the flower bed. "It's a good kind of tired. And I love looking at the cars."

"I know you do. You look excited dalking aboud'em."

Callie turned glowing eyes on to her aunt. "I found the one I want, and I should have enough saved to buy it before long."

"So much fasder?"

Callie beamed. "Oh, yes. You see, I'll have more money now."

Aunt Lily rocked back on her heels. "You god a big raise?"

Callie shook her head, nearly bursting with her news. "You know I got another letter from Mom. She said Riley has been working in town part of the time, and the bank note is almost paid off. Mom said I shouldn't send them any more money, to start spending it on myself. That means I can put that much more in my savings, and I should be able to buy that car soon—if someone doesn't beat me to it." She ran out of breath and had to stop her rush of words.

Aunt Lily laughed and picked up a trowel. She began to plant marigolds around the border of the bed. "It sounds like you may be heading home soon."

"Not until I get my car," Callie declared. "Oh, there's one more thing. Mom said Dad got a real deal and bought a used car from the Gentrys."

"Gentry. Habben'd I heard that name before?"

"They own the Chevy dealership in town."

"I see." Aunt Lily leaned back on her heels to study Callie's face. "Dese owners are good people den?"

"Oh, yes. They're community leaders and honest business people. Their son even lets us use an empty room in the back of the business for our community swap meets." She explained how it worked.

Aunt Lily jabbed at the soil. "And dis son got involved how?"

"He donated groceries from the very beginning. Then he began to do other things." Callie described some of them while working alongside her aunt.

"He sounds like a special young man. You sound habby when you speak ob him."

"Trace is that."

Another bout of sneezing overtook her aunt.

"I'll finish planting these if you'll go inside where you can breathe."

Aunt Lily pulled a hanky from her pocket and wiped her nose and watery eyes. She got to her feet. "I dink you're ride. I been out here long 'nuff. Dank you for 'elping."

Callie watched her aunt walk away and fought the fresh wave of loneliness that mention of Trace had brought.

Was she making a mistake? Should she go home? The family could use her help around the place, but they could also use a car. No, wait. They didn't need one. Dad had a car now.

Yet the thought of home filled her mind. Home. Where was home? Her parents' house was no longer her home. This house where she stayed was her aunt's home. She didn't have a home. Where did she belong?

She couldn't run back to Deer Lick just because she wanted to see Trace. If she gave up her job and went back, she became another mouth for her parents to feed—

without a job. And Trace might have forgotten her, or found someone else. He had said he cared for her, but that didn't mean he wanted to marry her.

If she knew for certain that Trace did want her, what would she do? The very possibility made her too weak to venture an answer. All she felt certain about was that a car would give her more independence, the freedom to roam, or go home if she chose. She had the means in sight, so the only thing that made sense was to stay with her job.

Lord, I've been focused on work for so long that I can't stop doing it. Help me. Let me know if I'm doing the right thing.

That week Callie bought a new dress for Easter. It made her feel extravagant, but she wore it with pride at having achieved one of her goals. *There's nothing wrong with homemade clothes, Lord. But it's such a luxury to not have to cut and stitch, to rip out mistakes and res-titch. Forgive me if I'm being lazy and selfish.*

After the Easter service at her aunt's church—she still thought of the little church back at Deer Creek as her church—Callie ate lunch with Aunt Lily before going to their separate rooms. Callie picked up her purse and sat on the edge of the bed. She took out the money that would have gone to her parents and added it to the little black bag that held her savings.

Lay not up for yourselves treasure upon earth, where moth and rust doth corrupt, and where thieves break through and steal.

Callie jumped as the scripture popped into her mind. She turned around. As she did, her vision landed on the half-open door of the closet. The sight of her new dress taunted her.

But lay up for yourselves treasures in heaven, where neither moth nor rust doth corrupt, and where thieves do not break through nor steal.

Had it been wrong to want a new dress?

For where your treasure is, there will your heart be also.

Understanding trickled through her. No, it wasn't wrong to want a new dress or a car. What was wrong was for those material possessions to be given greater importance than God's role in her life. She loved God, but she didn't always put Him first, trust Him completely to take care of her and her family. She knelt at the bed.

"Lord, I don't know what's in store for me beyond today, but I want to walk beside You whatever is in the future."

Chapter 15

Too much work. Not enough hours in the days. But Trace watched with pride and a sense of satisfaction as his home took shape. With Riley coming three or four days a week, and Arlie and Delmer helping as they could, the site felt more and more like a home. The extra work kept him bone tired, but it gave him purpose.

He stared at the building that still had a lot of indoor work to be done, his emotions a jumble. Could Callie be happy in this house? With him?

Should he write to her? He had considered it many times, but he feared he would not express himself well on paper. Even more, he feared rejection.

He had never been afraid like this. Flirting with the girls, even courting Joanna, had always come easy to him. Where had his confidence gone?

Lord, show me how to proceed. Nudge me in the right direction. Tell me when it's time.

When he opened his eyes, the first sight to meet them was Riley Blake on the roof, nailing shingles. Trace strode to the ladder that leaned against an eave and began to climb.

Riley looked over when Trace reached the top, his arm raised to swing his hammer. He paused in midair. "What's on your mind?"

The guy seemed to sense Trace's inner turmoil.

"Are you going to tell me how to find Callie?"

Riley lowered the hammer and grinned. "All you had to do was ask."

Trace considered the words. "Had to ask, huh?"

Riley nodded. "I been wondering if you ever would."

Trace waited, but Riley just sat there looking smug.

"Well," he huffed. "Are you going to tell me or not?"

Riley laughed. "You poor sap. You got it bad. So, yeah, I'll tell you."

Monday morning Callie went to work in a peaceful frame of mind. Money and buying things no longer held priority. If God wanted her to ride, He would provide the means. In the meantime, He had provided her with good health and two strong feet. She would walk and be content. Better than that, she no longer felt resentful at the financial circumstances she had been forced to endure all her life. God had control and knew what she needed. *Thank You, Lord, for always being there for me, no matter what.*

They only had a smattering of customers at the restaurant all day, but a quartet of diners lingered well past the end of Callie's shift. By the time she emerged from the building it was seven o'clock, and the sky was beginning to darken. She breathed in the fresh spring scents and basked in the pleasant duskiness.

As she headed up the sidewalk, Callie spotted a car across the street that made her come to a standstill. The aquamarine Chevrolet Superior looked so much like the one that had been on display at Gentry Chevrolet last fall that it brought a rush of emotion. A driver sat behind the wheel, but all she could see was the back of his head.

Suddenly he opened the car door and got out. Callie resumed motion, not wanting to be caught staring. Then she froze midstride and looked closer. Her heart leaped into her throat. She couldn't breathe—and it had nothing to do with pollen. She gulped as the man came across the street toward her.

"Trace," she whispered, unable to believe her eyes. Then her feet acted in place of her brain and carried her toward him. She got to the middle of the street and skated to a stop to keep from throwing herself into his arms.

He walked right up next to her and smiled into her face. "Hello, Callie. Your aunt told me where to find you."

"But…but why are you here?" she stammered, dizzy from the remembered spicy scent drifting from him.

He looked around at where they stood. "I think we should find a better place than the middle of the road to discuss it." He took her hand and led her back the way he had come.

Callie walked as if in a dream. This could not be real. Trace could not be here. He was back in Deer Lick, selling cars and causing female hearts to flutter. She would wake up at any moment.

They rounded the aquamarine car and stopped next to the driver's door.

"I brought you something."

Her heart thudded in alarm. He had brought bad news. "What's wrong? What happened? Did someone get hurt at the mill?"

He placed a hand on her shoulder. "Nothing's wrong. I hope. Like I said, I brought you something."

A cautious quality in his speech made her realize that he was nervous. The realization calmed her.

His eyes searched hers, his head at an angle that gave her a direct view of his expression. He reached back and drew something from his hip pocket, a folded sheet of paper, and handed it to her.

Callie reached out tentatively and accepted it. A letter?

"Look at it," he said when she just stood there.

With trembling fingers she unfolded it, and her name jumped out at her from a document. She looked back to the top of the sheet and read it. When she finished, she reeled back against the car, the strength draining from her legs. Trace looped his arms around her shoulders and pulled her to him to keep her from falling.

Callie looked up at him, her mouth moving soundlessly. Then she tried again. "This is the title to that car."

He nodded and reached into his pants pocket. He pulled out a set of keys. "These go with it." He turned her palm up, placed them in it and pressed her fingers closed.

She blinked back tears. "Why?"

He didn't speak for several moments. Then he tipped her chin up and directed a warm gaze over her face. It lingered on her chin, her mouth and then her eyes. "So you can have a car."

Her words from their last conversation came rushing back at her.

A faint smile squiggled at the edge of his lips. "I didn't

have a clue how to buy you a new dress, but I have an inside track on cars."

A huge lump shifted in Callie's throat. "You bought me a car?" Her words came out wispy with disbelief.

He cleared his throat. "Along with a new dress, you said you wanted a car more than anything."

"But you didn't have to buy it for me."

"I know. I wanted to do it. I wanted to make you happy."

Callie was too overwhelmed to know what to say to such an act. But then her brain came back from the dead. "I can't take this. It's too much." She tried to press the keys and document into his hands.

He shook his head and refused to take them. "It's yours. Please keep it."

She went still. Disjoined thoughts tumbled through her mind. What was his motive? What did he get from such a generous act?

"What do you want?" she blurted.

Steely blue eyes sliced through her, and then she thought she saw a gleam of mischief enter them. "Would you consider sharing it with me?"

Her jaw dropped. "Share it with you?"

He nodded and put a hand on her shoulder. Then, before she could gather her wits enough to protest, he pulled her close. "Live with me. Share everything with me. As my wife."

The last words were spoken so softly Callie was sure she had dreamed them. "As your wife?"

He nodded. "After you told me you wanted a car, you said that you care for me."

"I want you more." Callie couldn't believe she had said that.

A wide-eyed glow of pleasure lit his face. "I love you, Callie."

The simple declaration stunned her. But he wasn't done.

"Will you marry me? Have babies with me? Spend the rest of your life with me? Come back to Deer Lick with me to do all that?"

Her heart raced and soared. "I'll do all that, and even let you ride in my car once in a while—if you'll kiss me."

He laughed. And then bent his head. The lips-to-lips contact took her breath away, but it only lasted seconds. He drew back and took her hand. "Let's get in your car where it's more private and pursue this further."

He opened the door, and Callie scooted under the wheel to the center of the seat. He got in after her and shut the door. Then he pulled her to him. "Ah, this is better. Now, was that kiss enough for an answer, or do you need further persuasion?"

Callie breathed deep, unable to get enough of his spicy scent. Emboldened, she tipped her head back and aimed a teasing look at him. "It's enough, but further persuasion would be welcome."

He cupped her cheeks in his hands and gave her a little grin. "Callie Blake, soon to be Callie Gentry, I see that you're going to be a tyrant. And I'm weak." This time his kiss lasted long enough to convince Callie that she was thoroughly addicted to his kisses.

When he drew back, she wrapped her arms around him and pressed her face to his chest, too overwhelmed to speak.

"How soon?"

A blast of reality hit her. She sat up. "My job. I can't just walk away without giving Mrs. Palmer a chance to replace me. She hired me when I needed a job desperately. She trained me, and she's been good to me. I can't leave her in the lurch."

He smiled. "I understand. How much notice do you think you need to give her?"

Callie thought fast. "Well, she lost her last girl without warning and was just putting out her sign when I saw it and applied. A week or two should probably be plenty."

He tucked her head back under his chin. "How about this, then. Your aunt invited me to spend the night on her screened back porch. I could go home tomorrow and come back for you as soon as you call and tell me that you're ready to come. Of course, I would have to take your car in order to get home and back."

Callie raised her head. "You ninny. I should make you walk just to be mean."

He chuckled. "But you won't."

She reached up and trailed a finger over his cheek and mouth. Then she turned serious. "I want you to put your name on that title with mine."

"After I get both our names on a marriage license. And a ring on your finger."

She hugged him. "I asked God to provide for my future, but I never imagined He would do it in such a wonderful way. I love you, Trace Gentry."

Epilogue

"Are you ready to go, Mrs. Gentry?"

Callie smiled up at her husband of a little over an hour. "Whenever you are, Mr. Gentry." She basked in his lazy grin that warmed her to her toes.

He entwined his fingers with hers and led her outside. Callie shielded her eyes against the bright May sun, barely aware of the well-wishers behind them in the doorway of the church. She had been amazed at the number of friends and neighbors who had attended their wedding.

Trace led her to "their" aquamarine car, which now sported Just Married on the windows with soap and tin cans tied to the back bumper. He opened the passenger door and assisted her inside. Callie smoothed the folds of her new dress, marveling at how God worked even in small details. She never imagined when she'd chosen this cream-colored dress with yellow trim in Springfield that she was buying her wedding gown.

Trace got behind the wheel and started the motor.

"Callie!"

Callie looked around to see Jolene racing toward them. She rolled the car window down.

Jolene leaned inside to give her an awkward hug. "Be happy, Callie. I'll see you soon."

"Thank you for all the help you've been, and for the lovely reception," Callie said as her friend drew back. "I'll do the same for you when it's your turn."

Jolene shook her head. "I don't see that in the near future, if ever. Dad and Irene need me, and I love teaching. Now you two get going." She stood back and waved.

Behind them, people cheered as they drove away.

Once he got on the main road Trace reached over and gave Callie's hand a squeeze. "You're sure you don't mind living in my tiny rented quarters until we can get a house built?"

Callie squeezed the hand back and released it so he could steer. "It may be a bit crowded, but you have kitchen privileges. We'll be fine, and I don't care where we live so long as I'm with you."

He grinned over at her. "Well said, Mrs. Gentry."

"How long do you think it will take to build the house?"

The lopsided grin he gave her stole Callie's heart all over again. "Oh, not too long."

Trace turned onto the highway and drove into town, cans clanking behind them. On each side of the street people grinned and waved. At the four-way stop, he turned and drove the length of Main Street. But when he got to the street where he should have turned, he drove on.

"Where are we going?" Callie asked in surprise.

"I want to drive around a little more, show off my new wife. And I have something I want you to see."

Callie thought she detected a mischievous light in his eyes, but she settled back to enjoy the ride. Moments later she bolted upright. "This is the way to your property."

He nodded. "You're a smart lady."

Nothing could have prepared Callie for the sight that met her eyes when he pulled into the clearing and stopped the car. Nestled in the tree-cleared five acres sat a neat white frame house with a rail-enclosed porch wrapped around two sides of it.

Speechless, Callie turned an accusing look on Trace. "You already had this built before I came home and didn't tell me."

His eyes sparkled in satisfaction. "It wasn't an easy secret to keep."

A suspicious thought swirled in Callie's brain. "Is this where Riley has been working?"

"This is it. I asked him not to tell you so I could surprise you. Your dad and Delmer helped some, too, especially recently. Your dad built our kitchen table and chairs. If you hadn't been so busy these two weeks since you came back, you probably would have figured it out."

Callie burst into tears and threw her arms around his neck. "Trace Gentry…you…are…the…most wonderful… man in the…in the world," she blubbered.

He wrapped his arms around her and held her tight. "I hope you still feel that way fifty years from now." He buried his chin in her hair. "I love you, Callie."

She pulled back and looked up into his face. She wiped

tears from her face, but they kept coming. "Oh, Trace, I'm so happy I can't stand it. But you've done so much for my family and me. I can never do so much for you."

He gazed down into her eyes. "God has done so much for me. He gave me you, the best I could ever ask for in a wife. All I want from you is your love, and for you to live with me in this house."

Callie wiped her eyes again and stared over at her new home. "I love you, Trace. You've been in my heart for years. You'll always be there. I would love to live in this house with you."

"The house is all there is right now. Together we can add outbuildings and whatever else we need."

Of one mind, they shared a kiss of love and promise. Then Trace took her hand and opened the car door. "Let's go inspect it."

Together they walked toward their future.

* * * * *

REQUEST YOUR FREE BOOKS!

2 FREE INSPIRATIONAL NOVELS
PLUS 2
FREE
MYSTERY GIFTS

Love Inspired™

YES! Please send me 2 FREE Love Inspired® novels and my 2 FREE mystery gifts (gifts are worth about $10). After receiving them, if I don't wish to receive any more books, I can return the shipping statement marked "cancel." If I don't cancel, I will receive 6 brand-new novels every month and be billed just $4.74 per book in the U.S. or $5.24 per book in Canada. That's a savings of at least 21% off the cover price. It's quite a bargain! Shipping and handling is just 50¢ per book in the U.S. and 75¢ per book in Canada.* I understand that accepting the 2 free books and gifts places me under no obligation to buy anything. I can always return a shipment and cancel at any time. Even if I never buy another book, the two free books and gifts are mine to keep forever.

105/305 IDN F49N

Name _____ (PLEASE PRINT)

Address _____ Apt. #

City _____ State/Prov. _____ Zip/Postal Code

Signature (if under 18, a parent or guardian must sign)

Mail to the Harlequin® Reader Service:
IN U.S.A.: P.O. Box 1867, Buffalo, NY 14240-1867
IN CANADA: P.O. Box 609, Fort Erie, Ontario L2A 5X3

**Are you a subscriber to Love Inspired books
and want to receive the larger-print edition?
Call 1-800-873-8635 or visit www.ReaderService.com.**

* Terms and prices subject to change without notice. Prices do not include applicable taxes. Sales tax applicable in N.Y. Canadian residents will be charged applicable taxes. Offer not valid in Quebec. This offer is limited to one order per household. Not valid for current subscribers to Love Inspired books. All orders subject to credit approval. Credit or debit balances in a customer's account(s) may be offset by any other outstanding balance owed by or to the customer. Please allow 4 to 6 weeks for delivery. Offer available while quantities last.

Your Privacy—The Harlequin® Reader Service is committed to protecting your privacy. Our Privacy Policy is available online at www.ReaderService.com or upon request from the Harlequin Reader Service.
We make a portion of our mailing list available to reputable third parties that offer products we believe may interest you. If you prefer that we not exchange your name with third parties, or if you wish to clarify or modify your communication preferences, please visit us at www.ReaderService.com/consumerschoice or write to us at Harlequin Reader Service Preference Service, P.O. Box 9062, Buffalo, NY 14269. Include your complete name and address.

LIDIR13R

REQUEST YOUR FREE BOOKS!

2 FREE INSPIRATIONAL NOVELS
PLUS 2
FREE
MYSTERY GIFTS

Love Inspired.
HISTORICAL
INSPIRATIONAL HISTORICAL ROMANCE

YES! Please send me 2 FREE Love Inspired® Historical novels and my 2 FREE mystery gifts (gifts are worth about $10). After receiving them, if I don't wish to receive any more books, I can return the shipping statement marked "cancel." If I don't cancel, I will receive 4 brand-new novels every month and be billed just $4.74 per book in the U.S. or $5.24 per book in Canada. That's a savings of at least 21% off the cover price. It's quite a bargain! Shipping and handling is just 50¢ per book in the U.S. and 75¢ per book in Canada.* I understand that accepting the 2 free books and gifts places me under no obligation to buy anything. I can always return a shipment and cancel at any time. Even if I never buy another book, the two free books and gifts are mine to keep forever.

102/302 IDN F5CY

Name	(PLEASE PRINT)	

Address		Apt. #

City	State/Prov.	Zip/Postal Code

Signature (if under 18, a parent or guardian must sign)

Mail to the Harlequin® Reader Service:
IN U.S.A.: P.O. Box 1867, Buffalo, NY 14240-1867
IN CANADA: P.O. Box 609, Fort Erie, Ontario L2A 5X3

**Want to try two free books from another series?
Call 1-800-873-8635 or visit www.ReaderService.com.**

* Terms and prices subject to change without notice. Prices do not include applicable taxes. Sales tax applicable in N.Y. Canadian residents will be charged applicable taxes. Offer not valid in Quebec. This offer is limited to one order per household. Not valid for current subscribers to Love Inspired Historical books. All orders subject to credit approval. Credit or debit balances in a customer's account(s) may be offset by any other outstanding balance owed by or to the customer. Please allow 4 to 6 weeks for delivery. Offer available while quantities last.

Your Privacy—The Harlequin® Reader Service is committed to protecting your privacy. Our Privacy Policy is available online at www.ReaderService.com or upon request from the Harlequin Reader Service.

We make a portion of our mailing list available to reputable third parties that offer products we believe may interest you. If you prefer that we not exchange your name with third parties, or if you wish to clarify or modify your communication preferences, please visit us at www.ReaderService.com/consumerschoice or write to us at Harlequin Reader Service Preference Service, P.O. Box 9062, Buffalo, NY 14269. Include your complete name and address.

LIHDIR13R